Children of a Different Sky

edited by

Alma Alexander

KOS BOOKS

Bellingham, WA

PUBLISHED BY
Kos Books
© 2017 all rights reserved
https://www.facebook.com/KosBooks/
ISBN: 978-0-578-19666-4
eBook ISBN: 978-0-578-19666-4

Interior design and formatting by Mike and Danielle McPhail

Caelum non animum mutant qui trans mare currunt.
(*They change their sky, not their soul, who rush across the sea.*)
—Horace

Table of Contents

Foreword

The Idea, and the Appeal

There were voices in the wind. Wails, and groans, and screams; mutters and murmurs; sounds that spoke of anguish and of pain and of loss. And perhaps the loudest sound of all, the one that always followed those cries, the sound of silence—of absolute resignation and a giving up of hope, on the part of the dispossessed who drift across our world, and of a monumental helplessness, on the part of those who stand and watch and think they can do nothing to help.

When the idea came to me for this anthology on refugees, on immigration, I turned to a new thing in the world of publishing and telling stories—crowdfunding. If this charity collection, with its proceeds earmarked for the purposes of helping the least fortunate amongst us, was going to take wing... it was going to take a village. It was going to take a world. It was going to take a clarion call, to break that silence.

To that end, I put together a campaign for a crowdfunding platform with this appeal:

> *Hello, my name is Alma Alexander... and I am one of the unmoored.*
>
> *I have been lucky enough in my lifetime not to have been one of those truly adrift—I have never been forced out of a home, or a country, or made to go to strange places I could not understand, against my wishes, terrified and frozen.*
>
> *But I did leave the country of my birth aged 10, never to return there permanently to try and re-connect the severed*

roots. It no longer even appears on the world's maps under the name it bore when I was born. This does not mean I ceased to love it—it is where the bones of my ancestors are buried, where their ghosts walk yet if such things can be; this is the place where the river I love so much runs eternally between shores of mud and thistle and weeping willow, the place where a sliver of my spirit lives still, lives always. And I understand, on that visceral level, what it means to be FORCED to leave a place one calls home.

I feel for the children whose early—whose *only*—memories involve bombs and fire and fury and guns and bullets and dust and blood and loss and grief. I feel for the emptiness I see blossoming behind their eyes, underneath the pain, the inability to understand why such things can be. I understand the way an older child might feel when torn apart from those first precious friendships with one's peers, from the security and warmth of a family home; when witnessing the carnage of a hot war blowing up around them, none of their doing, something that they can do absolutely nothing about and that is completely capable of destroying everything they have ever believed to be true, like a dragon breathing a plume of flame on their lives and leaving ashes behind.

I watch these driven people who have lost everything climb on overladen boats which threaten to sink under the weight of frightened women and children and the few men *who are trying to save them. I can see pictures daily of the hungry, of the abandoned, of the families torn apart, of children sitting catatonic with pain and loss under streaks and smears of blood and dirt. I can see it all on the news, on social media, in headlines, across the world, every day.*

And I wonder what I can do. What I, and those like me, can do.

*We can tell stories. Not THEIR stories—those are theirs to tell, some day, maybe. But stories **like** theirs. Stories which will reach out and tell other people about the truth of their lives, through the "lies" of fiction, of fantasy. We can shine a light, we who create art, into the dark places of this* world. That is what we are for. That is what we do. That is what the best of us do, anyway. What we want to do. What we NEED to do.

This project is a collection of stories. Some by names you might recognize quickly; others, from writers who might have a more intimate, more visceral, connection with the subject matter, and of whom you might not have heard (yet). We are here to tell the stories. And when you choose to help us do this, with this book, with the collection of stories by the "Children of a Different Sky", you join us to learn, and to share, and to grieve, and to make sure that the least and the most bitterly lost amongst us are not—are NEVER—forgotten.

Back in the land I come from, there is a beloved poet called Aleksa Santic, and a beloved and well known poem entitled, "Ostajte ovdje"—"Stay Here". Young children of my heritage and culture know these lines—they are engraved on the souls of the humans of my nation. They are these:

> Ostajte ovdje—sunce tudjeg neba
> Nece vas grijat k'o sto ovo grije.
> Gorki su tamo zalogaji hljeba
> Gde svoga nema i gde brata nije.

Loosely translated, with poetic license, they read:

> Stay here—the sun of a foreign sky
> Will never warm you like this one in your own heaven
> Bitter is the bread in that place
> Where you're among strangers and not amongst your brothers.

We who were born under that sun, understand. There is no place like home, after all.

Like I said, I was never amongst those forced to leave such a place, which they knew, which they loved, where they belonged. But I left, nevertheless. And the poet is at least halfway right in that I never really feel more myself then when I (rarely, now) return to stand on the shores of *the river which flows past the city of my birth. I, too, in a distant and rather more comfortable sense than some are today... I too am a refugee.*

I wanted to put together a book of stories—stories which are about, and for, all those who found themselves on the road, alone, or holding the hand of a child, carrying only what was essential... and sometimes not even that. I wanted to use these stories to somehow help those who were adrift, dispossessed, wounded, abandoned, placeless, people who were losing countries and children and elders and bodies and souls.

The world was in pain—and I wanted to help. And one of the only ways I could help was tell stories, or gather together those who could. I put one of my own stories into this anthology, even though that is something that editors of anthologies seldom do, because I wanted to support the project at a more visceral level.

"Children of a Different Sky" was a child of that desire to help those most in need of assistance. We put the idea into the world. And the idea came back to us, and we made this book.

The Practical Aspect

We had to make a choice as to where we thought our donations would make a good impact and in the end decided on The International Medical Corps, an organization which has had teams on the ground providing medical assistance to Syrian refugees in Iraq, Jordan, Lebanon and Turkey. In the Turkish city of Gaziantep, not far from the war torn Syrian city of Aleppo, IMC helps run a service center for Syrian refugees that provides medical care, classes and job training. An IMC spokesperson says their work to help those affected by the conflict "is more critical than ever." The organization website says, "We assist those in urgent need anywhere, anytime, no matter what the conditions, providing lifesaving health care and health care-related emergency services—often within hours...and that's just where we start." Staff remain with communities, develop local partnerships by hiring and training local staff at all levels, and keep an eye on things to evaluate progress and ensure quality of aid.

From their website:

"We assist those in the world's poorest countries, often partnering with national and local leaders, to provide mmunities looking to build a better life for their people.

We are there for hundreds of thousands of displaced people, many of whom have lost everything and survive by clinging to all that's left: hope. We are there too for those who face less visible but equally acute emergencies such as malnutrition, the lack of clean water or a complicated child-birth. We work with partner agencies and local leaders to provide a broad array of services, often focusing on children and women with programs that improve maternal and child health and nutrition, provide for psychosocial needs and prevent gender-based violence.

Once urgent needs are met, we help communities in crisis-prone areas prepare in advance to withstand disaster should it come."

More about this organization at their International Medical Corps site, https://internationalmedicalcorps.org/

A portion of the profits from this anthology will also go to the Center for New Americans, a "community-based education and resource center for immigrants and refugees in Western Massachusetts". They describe themselves on their website as "a community-based, non-profit adult education center that provides the under-served immigrant, refugee and migrant communities of Massachusetts' Pioneer Valley with education and resources to learn English, become involved community members and obtain tools necessary to maintain economic independence and stability. Immigrants will acquire the tools to integrate economically and culturally into the community, and become self-sufficient."

More about the organization at their website at http://www.cnam.org/

These are just two of the many worthy organizations doing work with the dispossessed of our world. Here is a list of other potential recipients to any contributions you might feel moved to offer:

International Rescue Committee
https://help.rescue.org/donate/emergencies?ms

Mercy Corps
https://www.mercycorps.org/

American Refugee Committee
http://arcrelief.org/

Syrian American Medical Society
https://www.sams-usa.net/

Save The Children
https://www.savethechildren.net/

UNICEF

Doctors Without Borders

Acknowledgments

WE DID A CROWDFUND FOR THIS ANTHOLOGY.

The people and organizations who contributed to this project—at levels we called "Witness", "Activist Level 1: Grassroots Seed", "Activist Level 2: Fighter", "Activist Level 3: Organizer", "Marcher", "Leader of the March", "Speaker"—are gratefully acknowledged in the endeavour to bring this anthology to life:

Janka Hobbs
Patrice Sarath
Katherine Romberger
Dina S Wilner
Steven Saus

Dina S Wilner
Greg Hallock
Michael Jones
Patricia Burroughs
Frank P.

Bruce Sherman
Todd Ellner
Patrick Swenson
Karen Anderson
Stef and Aahz Maruch
Deborah Fredericks
Shirley Monroe
Debra L Lentz
Shanan Winters

Amy Carpenter
Rayna Lamb
Bruce Diamond
Elizabeth A. Janes
Gordana Curgus
Katrina Boyajian
Nancy Jane Moore
Colleen Reed
Manny Frishberg

Tim Dunn
Jaime Meyer

Paul Harwood

Kathryn McLaughlin
Sacchi Green
Liza Cameron Wasser
John C Wheat
Community Food Co-op

Without you, there would be no book. We are grateful for your support.

I wish to thank the writers who contributed their work to this anthology—Jane Yolen, Aliette de Bodard, Seanan McGuire, Irene Radford, Gregory L. Norris, Brenda Cooper, Joyce Reynolds-Ward, Randee Dawn, Patricia McEwen, Jacey Bedford, Nora Saroyan and Marie Brennan—for coming on board with this vision, and for giving me the incredible stories and poems that only they could give. They are telling the kind of story that touches the heart and stirs the spirit, the kind of story that is necessary to frame the narrative of the refugees and their plight with passion and with power. Their words are helping to provide direct monetary assistance to the International Medical Corps and the Center for New Americans, money which will go straight to the places where it can do the most good. But more than that, their stories serve as witness to a state of being, transcendent and strong, and I am very grateful that they chose to grace these pages. I am honored by their participation.

I also wish to thank people who contributed in other ways—Gordana Curgus, the artist who created the cover for the book, and Mike and Danielle Ackley-McPhail, for providing formatting and design expertise.

But most of all, I want to thank you—yes, you, the person who is reading this even now, who is looking at these words, who has read these stories and who may have been moved by them. All the profits from this charity anthology are going directly to IMC and the Center for New Americans who will use the contributions in such ways as benefit people in need—and you, by buying this collection, are the source of that aid. If you are holding this book, you are part of this reaching out with a helping hand. I am not going to say "part of the solution", because that is much bigger than any of us—and it would take far more than just one single little book of stories to solve a crisis this deep and this bitter. The cure for this disease is a greater task than this. But we, all of us, are part of immediate attention, perhaps just a temporary palliative treatment of a deep, deep wound—it may not be nearly enough, but it's something. We are trying to do what we can with what we have so that at the very least we can hold out a little bit of help, comfort, or hope. This is just a pause on a long, long journey—but I want to thank you for coming with us.

Alma Alexander
October 2017

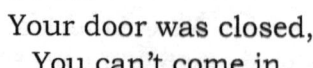

Your door was closed,
You can't come in.

Jane Yolen

Song for an Immigrant

JANE YOLEN

You made the sign,
You bent your knee,
You braved the storm,
You crossed the sea.
You held your child,
And one child more.
You made it to
The farther shore.

You made the sign,
You bowed your head,
You left your homeland
With its dead.
You crossed ravines,
You walked in mud,
You braved the deserts,
Swam the flood.

There were no walls
To keep you out,
But doors locked tight.
And haters shout.
The lady with the lamp
Has gone,
And yet your seeking
Still goes on.

The welcome mat
Sits all forlorn.
The safety net
Is tattered, torn.
A few doors creak
And open wide,
To bid you all
To come inside.

But Lady Liberty
Has fled.
Few offers of a meal
Or bed.
How did we come
To play these parts?
To close our eyes, and
Close our hearts?

So, when to heaven
We all fly,
Immigrating
As we die,
And try to enter
Heaven's gate,
St. Pete will say
You're much too late.

You're laden with
The worst of sin.
Your door was closed,
You can't come in.

...all they've left on the road's side, the photographs and the jewels and the sandalwood box holding useless visitors' cards from dead people—and everything they've lost hits her like a spike through the heart.
Aliette de Bodard

At the Crossroads of Shadow and Bone

ALIETTE DE BODARD

Then

In Vy's world, there is only the road.

She walks, ceaselessly, ignoring the ache in her legs and arms—a low, growling thing that never flares up, that never quite goes away. One foot after the other and another one—through the rice paddies and the forest, and the deserted remnants of villages. In the air, the dry, exhausted smell of sand and dust and the sour one of sweat and fear, grit that clogs up nostrils and lungs. Ahead, behind, the others—children, adults, her family, strangers, all with the same set to their faces—gaunt and taut, their clothes stained with dust and ashes.

Behind them—

No. They can't afford to look behind them.

Her throat is dry, her legs hurt—and on the road, those who didn't sleep keep walking, a ceaseless thunder of feet that's since long dried out of the mud. The sky is black, smelling of smoke, the sun a pallid, wavering miracle in the distance. Behind them is only the shadow of the Maw—a black cloud covering up the glint of lips and teeth, creeping forward, eating up trees and cities and villages, faceless, relentless.

"Here," Mom says. She hands Vy one of the rice cakes they made, back before they left Rong An, now so dry they're barely edible. The salty smell of fish sauce wafts up, so strong it's almost intolerable. "Eat up, and we'll start up again."

"What about you?" Vy asks.

"I already ate."

Adults always think they're so good at lying, but they're not. But Vy's found the key to turn that particular lock. She breaks the rice cake in three parts, and nibbles the first one slowly and deliberately. When Mom's attention has wandered back to little Huong—the baby nestled on her chest, hands scrabbling at she desperately suckles to get the milk flowing—Vy hands back the second third. "Here. For Huong."

Mom makes a face that hovers between pride of Vy and fear for her, but doesn't say anything. "She's right, lil'sis," Second Aunt says. "The baby needs it."

"I've kept a bit," Vy says, holding up the last third. She keeps a bright and insincere smile plastered to her face. Mom would see through it in a heartbeat, if she was well rested.

Mom frowns. "All right," she says. "But keep that one."

Vy slips it in her sleeve, wordlessly. She'll find a way to smuggle it to Second Aunt or Mom later, when they inevitably lose track of what she's kept for herself.

They're falling behind, Vy knows: because Mom and Second Aunt have a baby, because Vy is at that awkward age of eight, when she's too slow, but too heavy for an adult to carry. Three days ago, the family with them, the one with a child about the same age as Vy, rested on the edge of the Maw—because they had to, because they couldn't walk fast enough anymore. Mom thinks Vy didn't hear anything, and Vy didn't contradict her—but she woke up to a crunch of bones in the night. She looked: a fraction of a second only, caught the gleam of fangs in the Maw, a hundred thousand mouths covered by the darkness; and the sheen of blood and bones, swiftly swallowed up.

She's not scared. She can't afford to be scared. She has to be strong, to survive. But more importantly, to make sure the others make it to the border: to the wall defended by the Empire's alchemists—to a land without the war, without the Maw.

An explosion, somewhere in the distance. Vy tenses, ready to run on jellied legs, but it's only a government drone obliterated by three smaller rebel ones.

While Mom eats, Vy helps Second Aunt change Huong. The baby wriggles and smiles, and for a moment the world isn't grey or exhausting or ringed with fear—for a moment only, everything breathes out and opens, and a tight feeling of warmth spreads to fill the emptiness in Vy's chest. She tickles Huong, once, twice—all she dares to do. She expects Second Aunt to tell her off, but

Second Aunt doesn't speak; merely looks at the baby with an exhausted smile on her face.

"Time to go," Mom says. She straightens up her hair, wrapping it in a loose topknot, and Vy helps her wrap Huong in a scarf on her chest. Mom smells, faintly, of sandalwood and peony—a perfume that's souring into sweat and sickness as time goes by. Second Aunt shoulders the bag with the food—they've since long left everything else that might have mattered on the side of the road, all the pretty jewelry, all the letters from the dead—the box of sandalwood with the Double Happiness character, which used to contain the visitors' business cards, lifelines in times of war. Vy has kept her scuffed tiger toy, and Mom the picture of Mama from before the war, the second mother Vy barely remembers—but what's left is food and baby clothes, and not much else.

And then they're back on the road, slipping in between a family of Dao nomads and a group of Ho, now all indistinguishable, spattered in mud and dust and blood. The four women in front of them alternate to carry an old grandmother—it's a miracle they've made it this far without falling behind. There are no children of Vy's age, not anymore, and if there were she doesn't have the energy to talk, though Second Aunt is soon keeping up a steady patter of gossip with the four women, asking where they're from and how it's been for them.

"Lao Song, on the border..."

"The rebel alchemists dropped bombs on the village..."

"The Maw..."

Vy hugs Tiger against her, and keeps walking. The clouds are swallowing up the sun, nibbling at it like ten thousand teeth; it feels as though night is coming, even though it's broad daylight. She can't resist turning, just for a moment—just enough to catch a hint of the Maw from the corner of her eye—a black shadow spreading like ink stains across the landscape, and a gleam when it moves, and the smell of chewed-on, rotten meat.

When she turns back to face the right way, she sees something that wasn't there before, a flash of red by the side of the road. A red tunic and white trousers—and the woman wearing them, standing and staring at her.

Now

Vy has always known she would return, and always known how hard it would be.

Back then, the road they had walked on seemed endless. Now it's a short trip, except that that it's hard to get there.

Vy had to come on foot from the border of the Empire, begging soldiers to take her a little way in, and then making her way through the arid wilderness, sweat trickling down her back, dripping into her clothes. Her throat is dry; the water in her canteen tasting stale and too warm to be refreshing. The heat pierces the thin soles of her shoes like spears. As far as she can see, nothing: a desert with no people, no trees, no birds.

Where the Maw chewed, nothing will grow: it's just ashes left, and things that crunch underfoot. Vy could tell herself she walks on grit and sand, but she's older now, and she's meant to face the past. Bones. She walks on a carpet of bones: of gnawed-on shards, of broken arms and legs, of skulls cracked open and finger knuckles scattered like some nightmarish children's games. From time to time, buildings by the side of the road: deserted villages, houses open to the sun and rain—the Maw ate anything organic, but not stone, or wood, or wattle-and-daub.

Vy looks up, into the sky. Blue and cloudless, and a shining sun. It should make everything easier—tell her that the horrors are gone, that she's safe now.

Such lies adults tell themselves.

Ahead lies Rong An, the city of her birth—the compartment where she grew up, memories of cavernous spaces under tables, of the smell of garlic and fish sauce—and of bombs falling like rain on metal roofs, new year's yellow garlands going up in ashes and smoke—and the Maw.

Even now, they don't know who used the Maw, whether it was the rebels, or the government, or their imperial allies. In the wave of war crimes trials—theatrical, stage-managed affairs that seem to comfort Huong, but do nothing for either her or Mom—no one will admit to making or triggering it. All she remembers is how it started: how the sky curdled into blackness, the streets washed away, the market stalls swallowed up with a crunch of teeth and knives. How it grew slowly at first—a fist of shadow in the heart of the city, while they worried about bombs and riots and empty rice jars—and then spread faster and faster as it consumed more and more.

It's gone now, or so they told Vy. Stopped at the border with the Empire by the wall the alchemists have built—and, with nothing to feed on but itself, the Maw faded away, but not before it ruined the land past mending.

Gone.

Vy's hands have shut into fists—all she can see is dark skies above her, and she remembers the sheen of oil and metal in the blackness at their heels—her shoulders aching with the strain of not looking, of always walking ahead. And the years afterwards: the refugee camps with chlorine-laced water and boiled, taste-less rice—the adults' quiet and exhausted conversations about what they'd do, if the Empire decided to send them all home. The nightmares of finding the Maw on sidewalks and gardens that woke her up, gasping. The years in the Empire—the people shouting at her for stealing jobs and food, the well-meaning, barbed condescension of her co-workers, telling her how grateful to be for her rescue.

It will be all right. She doesn't need to go all the way to Rong An, all the way into the birthplace of the Maw. Just far enough to bring the loop to a close. She looks at the road again, trying to parse faded and imprecise memories. Every day seemed the same, when she was eight—is this where she first saw the woman by the side of the road?

Close enough.

A voice, in her mind. "You're shaking, and your heartbeat is well above normal." Lan says.

"Did you—"

"Put a tracking spell on you?" Her wife sounds amused. It's a simple spell: triggered by Vy's heartbeat, and the only reason it works with both of them so far apart is because of the golden necklace Vy wears around her neck—a wedding present, a deeper connection between her and Lan. "I'm an alchemist, lil'sis," Lan says. "What do you think I do for a living?"

Bomb cities, Vy wants to say, but it's unfair. They've talked about the past; about what each of them did and didn't do—what they let happen and what they didn't. Neither of them sleeps well at night. Lan makes her amends volunteering at a Buddhist kitchen, and even before the end of the war she was spearhead-ing rescue efforts for refugees. Vy—Vy just wakes up, gasping, shuddering at memories of the Maw.

The war has been over for twenty-three years now; it's been twenty-five years since she walked past the border wall and entered the empire's refugee camps.

Twenty-five years since she saw the woman from the future.

"You can still come home," Lan says. Behind her, she can hear the twins Bach Cuc and Bach Dao giggling, banging toys against the tiles of their kitchen. Thanh Yen seems so far away, the city with its wide tree-lined avenues a mirage, a years-long dream she's come up with on the road, to keep her mind from wandering. "You could—" Lan doesn't speak, for a while, and when she does, her voice is quiet. "You don't have to do this."

"I really do," Vy said. For twenty-five years she's lived with the knowledge of this, like a sword over her head: that, at some point, she would come back to the road—that she would speak to her former self—give her the hope that kept her walking.

"You don't even know who you saw," Lan says. It's a well-practised argument, one they've had time and time again, Lan's hands smelling of cut garlic and fish sauce, with the wind blowing, softly, in the trees of their gardens. "You've thought about it and come to this conclusion it must have been your elder self, but you can't be sure. And even if you're right—you could still walk away. What do you think you'll do, if you don't speak to Younger Vy? Break the fabric of time? Things will rearrange themselves. They always do."

If there's one lesson Vy has learnt on the road, it's the opposite. Things don't rearrange themselves. Doing nothing—not walking, not helping—merely got people killed... or worse.

Vy was a child then: a child who saw a woman in a red dress abruptly appear by the side of the road. They had a conversation together, one that Vy can't remember in detail—everything bleeding and merging together in the heightened fugue state of the road. But she remembers what it felt like, to know she had a future.

"You know I have to do this." She's woken up at night, listening to Lan's calm breathing and hearing only the crunch of bones on the road—going out to the twins' room, the floor under her naked feet the grit of the refugee camps, and seeing only bones beneath her daughters' chubby cheeks, and empty sockets beneath closed eyelids. "Call it... amends."

Lan's laughter is low, and bleakly amused. "You're not the one who needs to make amends."

"You've made yours."

"Can I ever?" Lan asks. There's no answer to this. There will never be. "At least think on it."

"I've thought for too long." And, with nothing but bleak amusement in her voice, "What do you think I do for a living?"

Lan is serious too. "I know," she says. "I'm not dictating what you can and can't do. But this isn't an exorcism, lil'sis."

Vy's not arrogant enough to think she can exorcise this place—even an immortal with a peachwood sword wouldn't make a dent on this road and its massed ghosts. No, she needs to do one small, simple thing: speak to a child and give her hope.

It should be small. It should be simple—and it feels like neither.

She takes a deep, shaking breath—holds it for a moment, until her lungs start to burn, distracting her from memories of the pain in her legs and in her stomach. Then she lets it go, and kneels, her hands going deep into the grit—scattering ashes and bones, and bringing up the breath of the earth beneath her feet.

There's almost nothing beneath her. The dragon coiled beneath the earth is wounded and broken, antlers broken, lustrous scales flaking away like so much dead skin—she feels their breath, slow and laborious. She can do nothing—it's far too late for her to intervene.

I'm sorry, great-grandparent. I need your help.

The dragon shifts, stretches. Vy feels, flowing through her, the slow rhythm of breath—the boundaries of her self stretching, fading—she's no longer locked in that body, in those memories, but part of something larger, the earth that always endures—the heavens above her, forever bright and unchanging.

It ought to be comforting—it always is—but here, in this time, in this place, it merely feels... weak. Inadequate, a child waving a flimsy stick to defend against alchemical fliers and bombs. Because she remembers the Maw, how it clogged the earth, how it covered up the skies until nothing of blue or of sun remained.

Vy starts walking. As she does, the road twists and changes in front of her—and a hundred, ten thousand translucent ghosts shimmer into existence, young and old, from babies to the grandmothers and grandfathers making their slow way out of the shadow of the Maw.

She can't look at the Maw. She's not meant to.—But it's there—the smell of rotten meat, the darkness that never ends, the teeth that bite, again and again, the bones that crumple upon the floor, the shadow that stretches all the way, coming to finish what it started, such a long time ago...

She can't.

Then

Vy stops, staring at the woman. She kneels by the side of the road, wavering and bending like a mirage. She wears an embroidered silk ao dai, without a trace of smoke or ashes; her face awash in a soft blue radiance that smooths out her features. She looks... otherworldly, like a goddess in a temple, or an ancestor returned to earth to bless their descendants—and yet somehow curiously familiar. Vy looks from her to Mom, and from Mom to Second Aunt—there's something in the woman's face, something in the way she holds herself, that speaks to both and to neither of them. A distant cousin, perhaps?

"Who is that?" she asks.

Second Aunt throws a glance to the side of the road, and then back to Vy. "Who what?"

"The woman." Vy points, hugging Tiger closer to her chest.

"There's no one. Don't be silly," Second Aunt says, shaking her head, and moving back to gossip with their neighbours.

If she were younger, Vy would tug at Mom's sleeves, and ask her the same question, but she's no longer that stupid. Instead, she watches Mom, and the Lao Song villagers—the way their gazes move to either side of the road, and then back again to the long ribbon of dust leading them out of the country. Their gaze never stops on the woman, and neither do they show any surprise.

They can't see her.

A ghost, a spirit? Why isn't she fleeing as well, then? She's looking at the road and the people passing her, her face twisted as if she were about to cry.

And why can Vy see her? She's not a medium or an exorcist—but perhaps that's how it starts—how you become one?

It's everyone for themselves and their own, on the road. Vy should pass the woman by; to look away as she looked away when Ngoc Bich died. Instead, she runs up to the woman, keeping a wary eye on Second Aunt and Mom. They're slow—trudging along the road, and the four women with them, and their grandmother being passed from hand to hand, makes them easy to find again, should she need to. Pain flares, briefly, in her legs, becomes a dull, familiar thing—and the world wobbles and contracts, every sound receding into the distance, and everything from the road to the skies taking on a yellow tinge. She's going to faint—she can't afford to, because she'll be left behind –she...

A heartbeat, and then it passes, though her legs still feel like they won't support her. "Are you all right?" she asks the woman. Every word feels like a struggle.

For a brief moment she thinks the woman won't see her, either. But then her eyes focus on Vy, and widen. "Child?" she asks. It's slow and hesitant, as if she'd been able to call Vy something else and changed her mind.

Adults are weird.

"I didn't remember..." Her voice trails off.

"You can't stay here," Vy says. She pulls at her—again, she's expected her hand to go right through, but instead it connects with an odd buzzing sound—and for a moment she's hanging, weightless, in something larger than her—it's not scary like the Maw, merely a feeling that someone, somewhere, counts her as their own. "Come on." Overhead, the sky is darkening again, and their own fliers have turned. Something is coming.

The woman gets up, stumbling—comes walking after Vy. "I can't..." she struggles, again, to get words out. "I'd forgotten it was so hard."

"You have to walk," Vy says, slowly, quietly. "People who fall behind—"

"I know," the woman says.

She looks... old and exhausted and ill, but in some odd way Vy can't define. It's not just the road, not just the fatigue—something more fundamental has given way in her. She lets Vy lead her back to the road—slipping in, effortlessly, some distance behind Mom and Second Aunt. The woman flicks them a worried glance.

"They can't see you," Vy says, patiently. She hugs Tiger to her, breathes in the smell of wet fur and the fainter one of sandalwood. "Or hear you. They'll just think I'm talking to Tiger." A low whine: in the distance are three fliers, and they don't look like they're from the government. Might as well ask: she's never believed in awkwardness, and there's so little place on the road for adult rules of politeness. "Are you a spirit?"

The woman's expression goes through an odd change. She looks at Vy again—that adult thing again, wondering how much of the truth she should tell her. "No," she says. "I'm flesh and blood, same as you. Just..." She takes in a deep breath. "This is going to sound impossible—"

Vy points back, to the Maw; to the fliers overhead. "No rules," she says, shortly. "You've been here long enough. You should know."

"I haven't." The woman's laugh is low and amused, and still completely wrong—hollow and drained. "Where I'm from, there is no road. Just a carpet of bones. The Maw ate itself out."

It makes no sense. "Where you're from—"

"The future," the woman says. "After the war is over. After—" She shakes her head. Surely, if the war is over—if there is no Maw, if there is food and shelter and more to life than the endless road—then she should be smiling and plump? But she's not, and that's scarier than anything. "After we get out of here."

Vy thinks, for a while. Not impossible or shocking, just... unexpected. She wants to say, *prove it*, but the woman wavers and fades from sight, her feet never quite touching the surface of the road, never throwing up dirt or mud. Her clothes are still pristine—she's not *there*, not with them. And yet...

Vy says, slowly, carefully—because it all sounds like madness, the stuff of dreams and fairytales and bedtime stories, the ones Mom keeps telling each night with increasing desperation—"I need to know—"

The woman's gaze focuses on her—again, that odd discon-nect, as if she'd forgotten that Vy was there. "—what happens?" She laughs, again.

Now

Vy had forgotten, but it's never been far from her, after all.

She's on the road again. Walking in the shadow of the Maw, which has grown and grown until she doesn't have to avoid looking at it, because she *can't* look at it, because the fear of what it'll do to her is enough to make her stomach clench, and for the acrid, burning taste of fear to flood her mouth—gnawed flesh and bones, teeth scraping against her cheeks and eyes.

Vy looks down, at the child she once was—grime-covered, pale-skinned, her cheekbones so large they swallow her entire face, her belly protruding from under her torn clothes—and that expression on her face—not the despair she remembers, but a simple dogged stubbornness.

She laughs. She can't help it. It comes welling out of her, a thing of broken shards that rakes the inside of her throat and leaves the salty taste of blood in her mouth. "We survive," she says. "It gets better." She thinks of breathless, sleepless nights, tossing and turning for a safety she can't find; but there are no words that can encompass this.

"You've been crying," the child's face is scrunched up in thought. Vy looks at Mom—so much younger, so much thinner than the steely-eyed woman she's become—and then back at her. The child turns, briefly—not long—towards the Maw. "You can see it, can't you? Why would you come here, if you don't have to?"

"Sometimes we get no choice," she says. *I had to give you hope*, she wants to say, but it's not the expression on the child's face—and perhaps not even what the child needed. She's looking at Vy with a frown, as if she couldn't quite believe what she's staring at.

Overhead, the drones have moved to meet the three fliers—the first shots hit the side of the road. She flinches. The child doesn't even move: she keeps a wary eye on them, on the road. "There'll be a stampede, if they do hit the road," the child says, with an assurance far beyond her years. "Have to watch out."

With every word, Vy could reveal things she wasn't meant to say—but does it matter, if the child—Vy—doesn't remember any of it? Would she start another timeline, if she did that—would she simply cease to be? All questions to which she has no answer—her teachers in the pagoda say time is like a dragon that eats its own tail, forever unchanging, all moments as one—that everything that will be has already happened, and the past cannot be changed any more than ink can be erased from paper without destroying it.

"You said it gets better," the child says. She shakes her head. "You don't look like it does."

She startles, stares at the child again. "I have children," she says, finally. Bach Cuc, slow and careful; Bach Dao, who'll pile up stools and steps and chairs if she thinks there's a chance of reaching a toy. A wife she loves. "A house with a garden, in the suburbs of a city, where the cicadas sing, come summer."

"Like they used to, in Rong An." The child shakes her head. She says, finally, "Younger Aunt—you know what happens to—to us."

"You live," Vy says, slowly, carefully. "Most of you." She stops, then. What good would it do, to the child, to know what awaits them—little Huong and Mom almost dying of dehydration, Second Aunt breaking her arm in the stampede to the border—the interminable, hollowed-out hours in the refugee camps with nothing else to do but worry and wait and pray?

"And get houses?" The child's gaze is on her again—weighing her, dissecting her. She didn't remember she'd been that way, at eight. "And families?"

She opens her mouth, then—heedless of the consequences on the timeline or whatever rot she's filled her mind with—she has to tell the child who she is, what happens—everything that will sustain her, on the road—that will keep her walking until she gets to the refugee camp.

And then she sees the child's gaze.

Not hope, not despair; but merely concern, and a faint, growing horror.

"You're..." The child stares at her, shakes her head. "It broke you. The road. The Maw—"

She escaped the Maw. She walked all the way into the Empire—she lifted herself out of the nightmare of the road, of the camps, of the city—"I survived," she says—and the words taste like blood on her tongue.

"But you never left." The child's voice is almost gentle—toneless and matter-of-fact, ringed with exhaustion.

It's that, more than the rest, which finally breaks her.

Then

Vy hadn't expected the look on the woman's face. It's like the day she broke Mom's favorite celadon plate, the only thing they had left of Grandmother besides the pictures on the ancestral altar—that same slow disbelief as the world rearranges itself, as it becomes clear that nothing can be undone or erased or walked back.

"I'm sorry," she says, quickly, words crowding themselves into her mouth before she can call them back. "I didn't mean—"

The woman's legs tense—she's going to run away, lose herself into the crowd. "Wait," Vy says, "Wait." She starts running; stops, as the world pulses and contracts around her, yellow bleeding out of the clouds overhead. Her legs feel pulped to jelly—she stands, shivering, shaking.

The woman has stopped, looking at her with horror on her face.

"I'll be fine," Vy says. She takes a deep, shuddering breath—finds the third of rice cake she's slipped in her sleeve that morning. It slides down into her belly, warm and comforting—not much, never much. But enough. "As long as I keep walking."

The woman's voice is low and spent. "It's not a life."

Vy shrugs. "It's not an entire life. It ends," she says; and then stops, realising what she's said—to a woman for whom this has never ever ended. "I'm sorry." She looks at the woman again. What could have gone wrong, that the road never left her—and then she tries to think of herself in the future; of a place where she can sleep that doesn't have her fearing she'll never wake up; somewhere where her legs don't ache anymore, where her stomach doesn't feel empty all the time. For a moment—an eyeblink, a heartbeat—it feels so wrong, so alien to her to be safe—for a moment only, she dances on the edge of the abyss, seeing the woman's future reflected in her own.

No. That way lies madness. She can't afford that; can't afford doubts or regrets. Keep walking. Never look back.

But—

The woman is looking at her as if she were dying of thirst, and Vy held water. But she has nothing she can give the woman—nothing that would change anything. "It'll be all right," she says, before she can think. She hugs the woman, quickly—that same odd buzzing filling her. "You'll be fine." And, because the woman looks so broken, so forlorn, "We left everything behind. Ghosts and memories and the past. You have to travel light." She thinks of their house in Rong An—of cicadas' songs, and wooden cars and dolls, of Grandmother's paintings, and the smell of apricot flowers and anise star in the yard, the cool touch of white tiles on her skinned knees, the distant voices of adults at table—of all they've left on the road's side, the photographs and the jewels and the sandalwood box holding useless visitors' cards from dead people—and everything they've lost hits her like a spike through the heart.

No doubts. No regrets. She pushes these where they belong—once, she'd have said the distant past, but now, she knows they're also part of the future.

Where I'm from, the Maw ate itself out.

One day, she'll come back.

Now

The child hugs her—it's an odd and disquieting feeling—she looks just a little like the twins—enough that she could be their sister or cousin.

"You'll be all right," she says. "It all ends."

It doesn't; and yet...

Vy watches the ghosts by her side; the road that's now bleached skulls and bones, but nothing else. Ghosts and memories and the past. She'd say they can't harm her, but of course that's a lie. Under her feet, the dragon in the earth stretches and turns, and she remembers she was the one who summoned the ghosts.

She stares at herself, at the inside of her wrists; at skin darkened by the sun, scarred by chips of rock and shrapnel—and hears, again, Lan's calm, reassuring voice, the steady sound of Mom cutting up aubergines in her small compartment in Thanh Yen, Second Aunt's laugher, the twins' excited babbling. "I'll be all right," she says, aloud. The road twists and fades, the ghosts leaving her—her younger self receding in the distance, consigned to confused memories and dreams.

Vy turns, slowly, to face the darkness of the Maw—it shimmers and fades under sunlight, transparent and unreal, a thing that died a long time ago. Beyond it lies the beginning of the road and the city of her birth; the house where they lived, the streets where she grew up; memories and keepsakes to be salvaged, ghosts to be exorcised, answers to look for—every choice spread out in front of her like pieces of jade on a jeweler's mat.

She stands up and starts walking through the ruins—away from the ghosts of the road, and back to where it all started.

We were told to count ourselves lucky
when all he did was banish us, rather than
set himself, sword and soul, against us.
Seanan McGuire

River of Stars

SEANAN MCGUIRE

THE RIVER OF STARS SHIMMERED BRIGHT AND CLEAN IN THE NIGHT-dark sky, each individual fish etched in a point of enduring light. The Maiden fled before it, her fins splayed wide, and the Fisher followed close behind, his star-sketched hands holding the bright illusion of his net. Clear weather, then. Good for sailors, poor for those who had no wish to be finned and scaled and sold.

Making final note of the stars and their positions, Kaida turned in the water, preparing to dive. Her father would be displeased to learn that they had so little cover. Storms were better than clear skies, at least when there were fishers in their territory. Storms drove humans back to shore, where they belonged.

Someone in the distance screamed.

Kaida froze, the spikes along her sides flaring in instinctive threat response. No matter that the threat was not to her: she could dive and be away from this place in seconds. But someone was screaming above the surface, and that meant humans were causing trouble again, causing pain and turmoil, in these, her family's waters. They had no right. They had no claim here, no stars to guide them. They needed to be reminded of their place.

Like a knife swept along the belly of a fish, Kaida slashed through the water, spines slicked flat, flukes driving her forward. The scream had come from the landwise direction, and so she swam that way, surfacing only once, to see that she was in the correct position. A ship appeared before her, brought into view by her own movement, and as if to signal the accuracy of her choices, another scream rang out across the dark sea.

Kaida frowned. This would not do at all. The humans forgot their place.

She swam the rest of the distance to their ship in an instant, reaching up to grasp the ropes which ran down its wooden bulk to the sea. There were hooks at their bottoms, intended to snare unwary fish. If she had come across this vessel under more casual circumstances, she would have cut their lines, reminding them that these were Nyimi waters, and not intended for the likes of them.

She left the lines alone. She needed them for other purposes. A mermaid grasped them, and a mermaid pulled herself free of the ocean's comforting embrace. A mermaid on two legs, swarming up the side of the ship like she had been born to climb the rigging and not to explore the depths of an unforgiving sea.

Kaida was almost to the top when she felt the first thin flickers of doubt. Perhaps she should have gone looking for her brothers, who were fishing these waters, and would be carrying good, sharp knives for the gutting and beheading of their catch. Landers respected knives as they did not always respect naked striped women, although most who survived an encounter with a Nyimi learned respect in short order.

Reaching up, she grasped the rail and pulled herself over, landing lightly on the deck...

...and found herself facing a circle of swords. A woman was tied to the mast, dark-haired, dark-eyed, and with several visibly broken fingers. She struggled against her ropes when she caught sight of Kaida.

"I'm sorry!" she shouted. "I'm sorry! They said they would kill my brother if I didn't scream for them! I didn't know!"

Kaida whirled to dive back over the rail, back to the sea, back to safety. The pommel of a sword caught her on the base of her skull, and she fell, and knew no more.

When she woke, it was in the hold of what could only be a human vessel. Only they built their ships so low, so tight, or allowed them to stink so. She could map the age of three separate catches, all of them slowly decaying in their barrels of salt and stench. Two of them were fish. The others...

Kaida closed her eyes. She would find the bodies, if she could. She would read enough of the stripes on their skin to chart their stars and guess their names, and she would swim every school she knew of until she found the one which sang a song of disappearance, of uncertainty. She would bring them certainty. It would cause them pain, but none as great as the pain of never knowing.

Too many schools swam now under that cold burden, their choruses never answered by the depths of an unyielding sea. More with every passing tide were forced to sing a song of sorrow.

Her school would *never* sing that song. She would escape this place, kill every cursed lander who swarmed the decks of this damned ship, and bring the songs of the lost ones home, as they belonged.

"Are you awake?"

The voice belonged to the lander with the broken fingers. Kaida was still deciding whether to answer when the woman sighed.

"Stupid, Cynere, stupid. She probably doesn't speak Docklands. I'm sorry, lady who crawled out of the ocean, I don't mean to talk to you in a language you don't understand. And I'm still doing it. I am a bad person."

"No." Kaida opened her eyes. "You may be a 'bad person,' as you say, but it is not because you speak to me. I make no judgment."

"You *are* awake!" The woman was tied to one of the pillars that studded the room. She looked at Kaida with obvious relief, features outlined by the glow of a small oil lamp. "They hit you awfully hard. I was worried they might have split your skull."

The blow had been delivered skillfully. Kaida was unsurprised to find her own hands tied, and scowled. It would have been a relief to rub her wounds, to take some of their sting away. "They would not dare. A dead Nyimi is a fortune in fins. A dead woman is suspect. Stripes can be feigned. Too much of our anatomy is...situational."

"You're Nyimi?" Cynere frowned. "I thought—forgive me—but I thought they were a myth."

"If I were a myth, my head would ache less." Kaida sat up as straight as the ropes would allow. It was nowhere near straight enough. The knots had been tied with dismaying awareness of her anatomy in both shapes: were she to transform, she would impale herself on her own spikes. "I do not like this. Did they tell you *why* they required your screams?"

"Only that they were trying for a better catch. I don't know what I thought—I'm so sorry."

"You did not know."

"They threatened my brother."

Kaida looked around the hold again. "Where is he? If you swim together, you should be kept together."

"They haven't let me see him since they took us on board. They said I couldn't be trusted unless they had leverage over me. We were supposed to be paying passengers. We're from Morada." The word was fluid and sweet on Cynere's lips.

"I do not know where that is," said Kaida. "But the sound of it makes me think it is very far from here."

"Yes." Cynere looked away. "It's beautiful. At night, the city is like a sky full of stars, and during the day, the flowers make the air taste like sugar. It's my home, and I'm never going to see it again. And I can tell by the way you're looking at me that you think my brother is dead, and maybe you're right, but I can't let him be dead in my heart until my feet are on the shore and every one of the bastards who put me here is bleeding out under a motherless sky. Do you understand?"

"Landers are strange and bothersome creatures, but vengeance, I understand," said Kaida. "You are the first lander I have met who seems to properly know the shape of it. Why will you not see your home?"

"Nyimi. You're a myth where I come from, but the myth says you have kings and queens. Is it true?"

"No," said Kaida dismissively. Then she paused, and corrected herself: "We do have leaders. Each school swims with its own authority, its own chooser of the ways. Without someone whose voice could chart a current, we would be forever arguing, and we would go wherever the tides would take us. Tides are not clever things. They should not be permitted to make such complicated decisions."

"What happens when one of your leaders dies?"

"Their children will take up leadership of the school."

"And will everyone accept this?"

"Not always. Sometimes, there is fighting. It stops, usually, before much blood can be shed. We are rare enough that we become, as you say, myth to some. We cannot afford to thin our own numbers through senseless fights. If an accord cannot be reached, the school may be divided. It has happened before. It will happen again." Kaida paused. Her disappearance might be the thing which triggered such a division. Her father loved these waters, which had been the home of his mother and his mother's mother, going all the way back to the Lady of the Tides, who had first offered the sea to the Nyimi like a jewel held in her hands. He wanted to stay. But her mother...

Her mother came from a school attuned to deeper waters, which came this near to shore only to reach the mating grounds. Her mother had been advising caution for tides. Losing Kaida might well force her to spread spines against her own husband, and when that was done, division would become inevitable.

If she did not escape this foul place, Kaida might be responsible for the end of her family.

"Well, hu—I mean, landers do something similar when there's a change in who rules us. The school splits. The new leaders keep the land and the cities and the good things and the gold, and the ones they think can't be trusted get driven out. Or they die. A lot of people died in Morada. The first one to die was our king. An assassin fed him poisoned honey, and he choked to death on the memory of flowers."

Kaida frowned. "My apologies for this your loss. Was he your father?"

"Oh, no," said Cynere. "My father was the one who poisoned him."

There was a momentary silence as Kaida puzzled through this sentence. Finally, she said, "My apologies. It seems I do not speak your language as well as I believed. You are saying your father is the one who killed your 'king'?"

"Yes."

"Then why...?"

"The king was a tyrant. He did as he liked, and never cared how much damage he did in the process. People starved in their beds. Plague ran rife. There was a distaff cousin with a claim to the throne valid enough to be honored, if the way was cleared. My father is—was—an assassin. Do you have assassins, in the sea?"

"No."

"He killed for money."

"Money, I understand." Kaida sneered. "The men who catch us do so for the money we can bring them. They butcher and sell us and rejoice, as if gold were any balance for a silenced song. I do not care for *money*."

"You need it on the land. If you want to eat, want to clothe yourself, want to live, you need money. The king didn't share the money he had with his people, and so the cousin who would be king approached my father and said 'if you kill him, it will be better.' And my father, the fool that he was, believed the words of a boy who wanted to wear a crown, and took his coin, and killed a king."

Kaida frowned. "As he was asked."

"Yes, but new kings don't tend to trust the people who killed the old king. My family, we worship at the altar of the seasons. We harm no one for faith, only for money. The new king, he believes in the ascendancy of the sun. He declared that all of our faith who were found within the kingdom walls at the month's end would be arrested, their assets seized, and their bodies put to the service of the crown."

"Your father—"

"Was branded a king-killer by the so innocent, so moral new king, whose solar god would never have sent him to the type of place where such men congregate. He was held up as proof that all of us who worshipped at the altar of the seasons were immoral, at best, and evil, at worst, our heads easily turned with money, our hands easily turned to evil. We were told to count ourselves lucky when all he did was banish us, rather than set himself, sword and soul, against us." Cynere lowered her eyes to the floor. "I have never known any home aside from Morada. My brother was set to marry a girl with hands as smooth as butter. She would have been my sister. I always wanted a sister. But weddings such as theirs would have been were banned even before we were turned out of our home, for how could the sun god allow one of his precious daughters to marry into *filth*?"

Her voice twisted on the last word, showing it for the echo it was. Kaida frowned.

"I am...sorry, you have been treated so by those who shared your waters," she said. "How did you come to this ship?"

"I said a lot of people died in Morada. When the new king spoke against his own subjects, there were those—especially those who saw themselves in service to the sun—who thought it was permission for them to do whatever they liked. They came into our homes with knives and fists and thought we wouldn't fight back. They forgot that even pretty gardens have thorns. We have been fighters for a very long time. We had only been decorative for a short while." Cynere looked up, and her smile was a poisoned spine aimed at the heart of the world. "My father died surrounded by the bodies of his enemies. He will be well-received by the season of planting, where even the graves bear fruit. My brother is young, not yet ready to be called to harvest. My mother's last wish was that I get him safely to some other shore, one that might be kinder, or at least might give him room to grow and bloom before he was cut down."

"And this ship...?" prompted Kaida.

"We dallied perhaps longer than we should have, preparing the fields." The way Cynere spoke made it clear that her preparations had involved blood and bone, and little else. "By the time we reached the docks, the new king's decrees had closed all but the worst doors against us. There were few enough ships willing to entertain granting us passage, no matter how much money we offered them. When this one promised us safe transit, even our own cabin, we didn't have much choice beyond trusting them."

"Landers lie."

Cynere frowned. "And mermaids don't?"

"I am not a mermaid. I am Nyimi."

"I thought—"

"To be a mermaid is to forget the waters where you began. To be a mermaid is to be reduced to a species, and not a people. I am a person. I am Nyimi. I swim beneath the stars of my ancestors, and they are the same, even if we have lost the spawning grounds where we first drew breath. I will go to the sea that waits for the dead, and I will see all those who came before me, and I will know them, because they will be Nyimi, as I am Nyimi, and they will welcome me home."

"Ah," breathed Cynere. "You are an exile as well."

"We are a species in exile." Kaida hesitated. "The way you spoke, of your family, of your father...are you an 'assassin' as well?"

"Not for lack of trying. I'm a killer, when I have to be, but I'm not the artist my father was."

"Can you heal, as well as harm?"

Cynere nodded. "I can patch a wound, if that's what you're asking."

"I am. There will be blood. I will free you, but I will need you to move quickly, or I may save your life at the expense of my own. I hope your hands will not be too great a hindrance."

"What are you—"

Transformation, for the Nyimi, was a simple thing built of complicated stages. Kaida focused on her arms, on the sharp spines which belonged there, the serrated, poisonous extensions of her will. They blossomed outward, slicing through the ropes even as they were turned back against her body. Cynere gasped. Kaida ignored her, more focused on using her now-freed arms to direct the spines against the ropes still holding her legs.

Blood cascaded down her arms and ran along her sides as she rose and moved to Cynere, crouching to slice through the other woman's ropes. It took longer than she would have liked, for she needed to be careful; a slip, and she would be wounded and the woman would be dead, neither of which would serve her well.

As soon as Cynere was free she rose, running for the wall. Kaida watched her go with a dim feeling of betrayal. Of course the lander had lied. Landers always lied. Landers always—

Cynere returned with knife in hand, dropping to her knees and beginning to cut slices off the bottom of her own skirt. Her broken fingers slowed her work, but did not hinder her completely. In short order, she had a series of bandages, which she wrapped around the puncture wounds in Kaida's arms, tying them tight without cutting off the blood flow entirely.

"I have heard you are poisonous," she said. "Is this true?"

"Deadly to you; a mild itching, to me," said Kaida.

"Good. I am...very glad that you did not harvest yourself on my account." Cynere tied the final knot and stood, the knife clutched in her hand. "Will you be all right until I return? I *will* return. You have my word of that."

"I will be fine," said Kaida.

She remained where she was, watching in silence as Cynere turned and began to climb toward the deck. It seemed a mean trick, sending a single lander to battle so many of her own kind. But landers were plenty and Nyimi were few, and she owed it to her father and her school to leave here, if she could.

A door closed. Kaida rose.

She made her way first to the barrels where the butchered bodies of her kin were packed. One by one, she tipped their contents out on the floor, spilling brine and blood as if they were the same, until the most precious catch these landers could ever hope to make was wasted, until she could run her fingers along the lines etched on clammy skin and see the stars these Nyimi had been born to swim for. She could not be certain of their names from anything as sketched-in as a starline, but she could see enough that when she spoke of them, their kin would recognize their shadows in her words. It was the best that she could do. Sorrow had never raised the dead, nor vengeance soothed the living.

Screams came from above, muffled and deadened by the wood. Whether they belonged to the fishers or to Cynere, she did not know. She hoped for the former. Cynere deserved to land a few blows before she was cut down. She had earned that much, and more.

Kaida turned her attention to the walls, where some doors were waiting, closed and latched against their occupants—if they had any. Perhaps one of those doors would lead to a hatch intended to be used for dumping offal into the sea, and she could make her escape before the battle's victor came down the stairs to claim her.

Behind the first door was nothing: an empty room, with shackles on the walls which she looked at and chose not to consider further.

Behind the second door were people. Some were human, including a young boy whose hair and eyes were like Cynere's, whose arm was broken and held stiffly against his body. Kaida blinked at him. He shied back, pressing himself against the bulk of a woman whose torso was as an unstriped Nyimi or a lander, but whose lower body was that of some vast land-dwelling beast, with hard shell feet and a long tail of tangled hair. The others in the room huddled behind the woman, who put her arms around the boy and narrowed her eyes in suspicion and threat.

"If you've come for a fight, you'll have one," she snarled. Then she blinked, seem see that the stripes on Kaida's arms and legs were not clothing, but natural coloration. "A...very naked fight. You're not here for a fight at all, are you? Who are you?"

"My name is Kaida. I was caught by the men who hold this ship. Another woman, who is called Cynere, has gone to explain to them why capturing thinking beings is beneath them. I do not believe there will be a second lesson."

The beast-woman blinked again before smiling. "Well, then, we'd best go help with the education, hadn't we?"

The deck was awash in human blood, red as sunset, running along the planks and mixing with the spray coming over the sides. At the center of it all stood Cynere, knife still clutched in her unbroken fingers, a sword—hers now, however she had acquired it—in her other hand. She was panting slightly, her head bowed forward, and the only sign that she had been the cause of so much killing was a scratch along the angle of one cheek, as delicate as the mark left by a single Nyimi spine.

The freed prisoners boiled up behind Kaida, pushing her aside as they rushed to seize the ropes, the wheel, and—in the case of the small boy with the broken arm, who cried "Cysi!" as he ran at his sister—Cynere herself.

Cynere looked down, eyes widening. Then she dropped to her knees and folded the boy in her arms, letting her weapons fall unheeded.

The beast-woman stopped next to Kaida. "A happy ending. Not so common, when dealing with a ship that preys on the fears and needs of refugees."

"There are no endings. Only changes in the tide." Kaida looked at her. "What are you?"

"A captain in my own right, when my ship isn't in dock being repaired. My name is Phillipa Fairweather." The beast-woman raised the eyebrow above her single visible eye. A black patch covered the other. "Or is that not what you meant, Nyimi?"

"You know us, then."

"I know these men were hoping to fill their hold with you, to sell alongside the rest of us."

Stripes on skin, flesh in barrels. "They caught enough of us. They will catch no more."

"True enough." Phillipa inclined her head. "I'm what they call a centaur, on the land. If you ever decide you've had enough of the waves, or enough of men like these butchering your kin and kind, we'd be happy to have you. Doesn't matter if you know sailing or ships. We can teach those things. What matters is you opened a door when you didn't have to, and maybe you could tell the local Nyimi not to throw things at us."

Kaida said nothing.

"Go to the shore, there." Phillipa pointed toward the distant light of a city, far down the slope of the shore, barely visible through the dark. "Ask for the *Jackdaw*, or the horse-lady who sails her. Anyone you find will point you right."

"Take her." Kaida pointed brusquely toward Cynere. "She can fight, but she is from a garden. She does not know how to grow wild."

"And what does a sea-girl know of gardens?"

Kaida said nothing, only turned and walked to the rail, pulling herself over it. When she glanced back, only for an instant, Cynere was watching her.

She let go of the wood and dropped, back into the waiting sea. There were songs to be sung, and families to be notified. There was mourning to be done.

And perhaps, when all those things were finished, there would be a city to seek, and a captain to speak to. Being able to speak to the ships, to speak for the Nyimi and be heard, might change things for the better. Might make these waters safer, and stop the songs of sorrow.

The River of Stars still shining brightly above her, Kaida dove, and was gone.

That's the natural order of things. It is natural for
humans to divide into two or more sides and go to
war to determine who should rule. The people who dwell
in the middle must be pushed aside to clear paths of
invasion. It is their destiny to become refugees.
Irene Radford

The Natural Order

IRENE RADFORD

1ST SERGEANT DORE, 4TH BATTALION, CHECKED THE LOAD IN HER pulse rifle. Enough for a dozen single shots or one short burst of rapid fire. Was it enough to control the mob of refugees waiting in line to exit the shuttle?

The vessel needed every atom of remaining energy just to get dirtside, overloaded with more than two hundred refugees, their twenty guards, plus the fifty member crew of the now that they had arrived soon-to-be-derelict space ship. Why would she expect anything left over to charge weapons?

The cargo didn't seem to care if the weapons worked or not. They'd seemed docile enough, loyal to the Natural Order of Things that had doomed them to become refugees.

Until those in power on Earth had decreed that the refugee camps were in the way of their invasion forces, so the camps had to go. Why not let refugees explore new worlds and breed new troops elsewhere to feed their never-ending need to fight each other?

The two current emperors decided the space fleet abandoned in orbit two hundred years ago was getting in the way of their missiles. So, solve two problems at once, send the refugees away before the orbits decayed to the point they endangered precious troops. A few hobbyists dug out ancient files and found a dozen planets deemed suitable for humans to breathe the air and possibly feed themselves. And if they survived, they could breed new troops.

No one mentioned to the troops and the ships' crews that it would be a one way trip, for them as well as for the refugees.

Those ships hadn't the hull integrity or the fuel to return to Earth.

"You there! No pushing. No crowding. No getting out of line," 2nd Lieutenant Bullé ordered at the top of his basso voice. It came out as a cultured bellow, worthy of an opera singer. Indeed, he'd trained to be the star of La Scala until the Emperor had decreed he must follow his father into the military. As the first son, that was his duty and the natural order. Frivolous careers were left to younger siblings.

1st Sergeant Dore, 4th Battalion, 7th Division, 12th Corps raised her rifle to rest on her hip, not aiming at anyone in particular, just letting the restless throng know she was ready to shoot if they got too out of hand. They continued to shift restlessly from foot to foot while they waited. Their lives were dedicated to waiting. That was the lot of the refugee. The natural order.

At last the shuttle touched ground on a newly found planet. Only drones had explored it, sending fractured and indistinct pictures back to Earth two centuries ago. The ship bounced and skidded, tipped on its nose, and flopped back, breaking two of the four wheel stanchions to starboard.

The people standing in line jerked forward, piling into each other. They screamed and flailed. Moans of pain pushed past Dore's eardrums, already mangled due to air pressure changes and screaming metal trying to stay intact on the too rapid descent. She fought for balance, found the deck canted to her left. With that knowledge she managed to establish herself upright. Then she waded into to the melee, pulling people off the top and setting them aside. The five uniformed people under her command followed her, doing likewise.

In minutes they had the people sorted and back into something resembling a line. Only the three at the front were seriously injured. Bullé had moved as close to the forward hatch as he could manage to stay out of their way. He looked about in panic until he spotted Dore. Then he righted himself, set his threadbare uniform to rights and ordered his sergeant to deal with the few moaning and crying injured.

Dore assessed a broken arm, a concussion, and a cracked rib. The first aid kit was at the rear with her personal gear. So she made the three sit in the front most seats, out of the way and promised them all aid and comfort when they'd disembarked on their new home.

Bullé took that as his signal to open the hatch. It irised open half way at the touch of his palm print and retinal scan. Then it halted. The entire vessel seemed to sigh in exhaustion. Bullé and Dore got in the middle and pushed. Eventually they got the door three quarters open, enough for two people at a time, and manually cranked down the ramp the rest of the way.

Fresh air rushed into the rank hold of the shuttle. Dore paused to fill her lungs and coughed it all back out again. It had been so long since she'd breathed anything but recycled chemicals that her body refused to acknowledge this atmosphere as anything useful.

Bullé leaped free of the cockeyed ramp and turned a slow circle, pulse pistol charged and ready. "Hold, hold, hold," he yelled back to the mass of people pressing to exit. Everything came to a jagged halt at the panic in his voice.

"Dore, this does not look like a refugee camp. We have green grass and trees. Those are reserved for the wealthy. We must blast a perfect circle down to bedrock and let charred dirt and dust fill it back in. Order the captain to fire all weapons!"

Dore, snorted. "There isn't enough energy left to recycle air let alone charge a blaster."

"But the natural order of things..."

"Doesn't work here," she muttered, not caring if he heard her or not. Then she sorted out the mass of people and pushed the first two out the hatch and down the ramp, followed by two more.

"Just like the ark," one of the refugees said to her with a smile. The first smile Dore had seen from these people in months of space flight.

"An ark," the woman behind him whispered. "We're an ark settling on a new world."

"Look, look!" cried a teenager at the mouth of the hatch. "A rainbow. Do they have rain on this world?"

"With all that green out there, there has to be moisture, rain or ground water."

"Hey, even the sky is green. We won't go thirsty here."

"And it's warm, but not scorching. Comfort."

"But... but we have no fence to contain you!" Dore could hear the rest of it, the mantra that was the only thing Bullé knew, echoing inside his mind: *That's the natural order of things. It is natural for humans to divide into two or more sides and go to war to determine who should rule. The people who dwell in the middle must be pushed aside to clear paths of invasion. It is their destiny to become refugees. Refugees must be contained so they don't contaminate...*

"Give up, Bullé. This is a different world. We get the chance to create our own natural order of things. Guns won't work." Dore threw her rifle as far to her left as she could. Then she grabbed Bullé's pistol and heaved it to the right.

Behind her the limited troops did the same with their weapons.

"We get to work together to make our new world whatever we want. We can farm and forage. You can *sing*! I can dance. We can live free and die free, without the shadow of war making decisions for us. *We* decide the natural order of this world, not the emperors back on Earth. We do."

She stepped out of the way, to allow people who were no longer refugees to stream off the ship and onto the green grass of their new world, free to establish their new home with no particular order to anything.

Dirty Raggs. The place stinks like cinnamon.
Gregory L. Norris

The Pillars

GREGORY L. NORRIS

MISTER ULMER ALREADY DIDN'T LIKE THEM, BEEBE'S MOTHER SAID. She paced the apartment, which grew colder, darker, as seconds dragged out with the weight of long hours and the Pillars stayed gray. Just another Ragg family living off government handouts and Pillar assistance, that's what Mister Ulmer would say.

"What's 'Pillar assistance'?" Beebe Magenta asked.

Her mother turned and fixed her with one of those looks, and Beebe realized she'd slipped up again; that Nelida Magenta hadn't spoken the words but had thought them.

"I'm hungry, momma," Beebe said, hoping a fresh argument might counteract an older one. "When can we eat?"

You're reading my mind again, Beebe heard, though in the graying light within the apartment, she couldn't tell if her mother's lips moved. But when Nelida spoke again, it was not to mention food. It was the words that ended every argument.

"Go to your room."

Beebe huddled on her bed, a tiny square of blankets on the floor set beneath a window cloaked in curtains fashioned from a sheet. The Pillar in the corner sat gray and silent. She scooted over, touched the transparent tube, and found the surface cold. Not icy, like in the summer months when the system absorbed heat and humidity from the air, more like a metal railing at her school where she and other Raggland kids gathered five times a week. Poor kid's school, she'd overheard more than once, whether the sentiment was spoken aloud or jumped out of the speaker's thoughts, like a bug alighting from the folds of a dark flower blossom.

"Are you in there, Ky'neika?" Beebe asked the still, gray tube.

Her imaginary friend—that's what Beebe's mother called the girl living in the Pillar—didn't answer. Beebe rapped the Pillar with her knuckles, though that was fated to get her punished if found out. The Pillars were not to be touched. As though to cement that warning, she caught parts of a one-sided conversation even before Mister Ulmer walked in—*they've got a kid, bet she's been messing around with the system again!*

A knock sounded on the front door in lieu of the sharp, chirpy chime of the bell. With the Pillars gone gray, nothing worked except Beebe's imagination. She heard Mister Malouf next door talking to himself, though the walls should have devoured the words, and the grinding of Mister Ulmer's teeth when he walked past the threshold and into the living room of Beebe's apartment.

Tasteless, he said, and though Beebe heard the thought she didn't understand it, because her mother hadn't offered him anything to eat, either.

What followed was more accusation—the Pillars had only gone in five years earlier, top-of-the-line tech, none of that Black Diamond garbage from the Ukraine. Made with pride right here in the Good Old Americas.

Dirty Raggs. The place stinks like cinnamon. Not sure what they did to the system, but I bet it was that kid of theirs—

"No," Beebe shouted, unable to contain the outburst, even if Mister Ulmer's claim had merit. "It wasn't me!"

The apartment fell silent again. The chill deepened, as did the darkness of the new night.

"Mrs. Magenta, I'll have to do a full restart to your system," Mister Ulmer sighed, and Beebe didn't need to read the man's thoughts in order to comprehend his mood. "It's gonna take a while. If that doesn't work, you and your daughter are in for a long, cold night. You may want to call a friend with a guest room, just in case."

"No, absolutely not," her mother insisted. *Nelida Jovan Magenta was no charity case*, she emoted in silence.

That, and she worked hard to pay for the place—the least she could expect was decent Pillars to keep it warm and run the lights, stove, and refrigerator. What she didn't say, though Beebe heard it as clearly as Mister Malouf's mumbles, was that they hadn't made many friends since escaping from the Ragglands. There were no guest rooms available, and no extra money to pay for a motel, even the cheapest out near the spaceport.

"We'll hope for the best," said Mister Ulmer.

The Pillars were out.

Beebe watched her mother's approach with a sense of familiar sadness. The candle Nelida carried reminded her of the one they'd lit for her father at the temple. That candle was long, thin, white. This was imprisoned in a glass jar. Still the flickering flame connected both. A representation of the soul, a kindly older woman had said, or thought, at the temple. She hadn't known Beebe's father, but how she and four other woman dressed in black had wailed for him and the others remembered on that day.

"So you can see," her mother said, bringing her out of the past and back to the moment. "Don't play with it."

Nelida set the candle in the jar upon the old wooden dresser that they'd been granted from the apartment building's 'still-good' cages in the top floor filled with castoffs from previous tenants.

"I won't," Beebe said.

"Promise."

She did, and crossed her heart. Her mother lingered at the bedroom door, and Beebe sensed all Nelida wanted to ask. Exhaustion made the thoughts difficult to link together and read clearly.

"Try to sleep," Nelida said, settling for that instead of saying something that would begin a conversation she did not want to continue. .

"There's no one to talk to anyway," Beebe said, and instantly regretted slipping up.

Her mother's eyes shot toward the dark Pillar. "You aren't going *there* again, are you?"

Beebe held her tongue.

"I asked you a question. *Ky'neika*. The girl that lives in there?"

Before she could muster an answer, Nelida about-faced and marched away to the other end of the apartment, where a second candle flickered.

Ky'neika was gone, Beebe sensed. Free. It was Beebe who had helped her escape her imprisonment inside the Pillars.

Beebe drew the covers up to her face so that only her nose extended past the corner, and then sandwiched her head between two pillows, just like Grandma Ella used to in that other life and distant place, in the Ragglands. Grandma Ella had claimed it helped her to sleep by cutting out all the noise and chatter. Whenever Nelida caught Beebe sleeping like her father's mother, she flipped out, cursed both humans and gods in the language of their birth, and ordered Beebe not to repeat the action. It was forbidden. Beebe remembered how Grandma Ella had been asleep when the fire broke out, asleep with her head between the pillows, the world and all its voices tuned out. Not even Beebe's screams had woken Grandma Ella from that deep sleep on that tragic day.

Only sleeping in that fashion didn't completely silence the world's voices and thoughts. Beebe just liked feeling warm and protected, and connected to Grandma Ella, who could also read other people's thoughts and had gifts she often labeled as curses.

Mister Ulmer was back, with his tools and replacement parts, which would keep her mother occupied. Beebe slipped deeper beneath the pillows.

"Let me remind you that this is the second time since you moved in," he said. He didn't sound any more pleased than during his previous visit.

"Which should tell you that the problem's with the Pillars themselves, not us."

Ulmer went into the usual spiel—about how clean-burning power after petroleum got phased out was more than a gift; it was a miracle that kept people warm in the winter, cool in the summer, and lit their nights against the darkness. It didn't simply break down.

With her head between the pillows, she listened to the theoreticals and gobbledygook his mind used to fill in gaps where the technology eluded him. Exotic energy particles. Limitless source. A dark thought floated past the structural schematics from which Mister Ulster took his basic knowledge: the Magentas had likely sabotaged the system out of spite. After all, they were from the Ragglands, whose desert sands had been squeezed dry of oil. But it wasn't even true, not really Their family had lived along the fractured coastline of Old Lebanon, Beebe argued in silence, where the only oil came from cedar trees and olives.

Limitless, yes. But the energy contained within the Pillars didn't burn as cleanly as Mister Ulmer thought, Beebe knew.

"What were you doing before the system went down?" he demanded more than asked.

"I was about to fix us dinner. I swear, we did nothing out of the expected. My daughter was in her room doing homework."

Which also wasn't entirely the truth, Beebe thought.

"It's so cold in here," Nelida said. "Can't you hurry this up?"

Beebe extended her nose out from the covers. When she exhaled through her nostrils, she saw her breath transformed into a curlicue of gray rising up, up, before vanishing somewhere between the space over the bed and the ceiling.

She thought of her father, Grandma Ella, and of Ky'neika. There'd been another man before Ky'neika who'd also lived inside the Pillars. Beebe's pulse galloped. She heard the frantic heartbeats as they throbbed in her ears, which helped to dull the other noises and voices around her.

She drew back the covers and focused on the candle's flame. Just like the one in the temple, representative of her father's spirit, burning warm and bright among the stars of Heaven.

Energy thrummed through the apartment, and the air shuddered. The Pillar in Beebe's room lightened from gray to a dull orange. The glow intensified, and the color purified to a sunny yellow.

"There," Mister Ulmer said. "You should be back up to full lumens within an hour, I'd say." *That quick enough for you,* Beebe heard the man add, bookending the private statement with a sigh.

Nelida voiced relief in silence, using a mix of holy and forbidden descriptors. Beebe removed the top pillow fully to avoid her mother's anger. The light thickened to gold. By the time her mother entered the room following Mister Ulmer's departure, the Pillar was white, verging on blue.

The air warmed. Nelida blew out the candle and studied Beebe through narrowed eyes.

"Beebe Magenta," her mother said in *that* tone. "Promise me that you had nothing to do with this."

Beebe drew in a breath. "No," she lied. "I did not."

"And what about your—"

Imaginary friend. A trick, a trap, Beebe knew, and wished the words off her tongue before they reached her betraying lips. Silence, however, seemed to confirm her guilt worse than reading Nelida's mind and answering her mother's questions.

Beebe's mother folded her arms and turned. In the warm blue light of the Pillar, the girl clearly saw the exhaustion on her mother's face, along with something worse she guessed was fear.

Heat infused the small apartment.

Beebe dialed down the dim switch on the wall above the dresser and, at first, a sense of relief washed over her. Mister Malouf from next door had stopped his solitary conversation, unaware his novenas were being heard by ears other than those of saints; Nelida slept, dreaming of a far-off place where a merry-go-round spun within a dense, protective wall of cedar trees according to the stark images Beebe saw secondhand; and the steady thrumming undercurrent cast by the Pillars pushed Mister Ulmer's mean thoughts from the front of the girl's memory.

She settled back on the blankets and again slipped her head between the pillows.

Hello.

Beebe's eyes shot open. At first, she waited, hoping the voice would go away.

Can anyone hear me?

Beebe held her breath.

Please, I don't know where I am. It's dark but I can see you there. My name's Margaret.

Beebe tossed the covers aside and hurried over to the Pillar. She set both hands on the dense transparency. Warmth crackled over her palms and fingertips.

"I'm here," Beebe whispered. "Only I can't talk too loud or I'll get in trouble."

Where am I?

"Our place, far from the Ragglands. You're in the Pillars now."

I don't understand.

"High-yield energy collector and distribution cylinder—that's what Mister Ulmer says. He's our maintenance man. I think you're the energy."

What? Margaret's voice broke on a sob.

"Don't cry," Beebe whispered to her new friend.

But why?

"Because, I think you're like the flame of the candle, Margaret. One of the stars in Heaven. Only the Pillars reached up and pulled you down."

I don't want to be here. How is it that I can hear you, see you, and that you can hear me?

"Like my Grandma Ella, I have a gift. I... I can release you... "

Beebe drew in a deep breath and waited for what she knew would follow.

Little girl, will you use your gift and help me escape from these Pillars?

"Yes," Beebe eventually said. "I will."

She gripped the Pillars and willed her new friend free.

"I want to fight."
"You have to live to fight!"
Brenda Cooper

Heroes

BRENDA COOPER

IT TOOK A LONG TIME, MANY MILES, AND A DEATH FOR ME TOUCH MY daughter, Lucienne. That morning, the one after the Russians overran Vancouver, Canada, there was three feet of distance between us but it felt like miles. She and I sat side by side on a hard wooden booth in the Sacred Brew Coffeehouse, my coffee cup and her hot chocolate both empty.

We both watched Juliette closely. Her lashes curled dark against her coppery skin, her gray-green eyes looked past us both. Lucienne fidgeted, glancing furtively at each of us, looking by turn angry with me and like she might want to jump into Juliette's skin and be her.

Juliette and I had already said the things we needed to. It felt awkward but sweet, like the mornings after she and I dumped our fear and stress in long, sweet lovemaking. I had used her to feel touched and noticed. She had enjoyed it. It had been release, never forever. One knows. We even said so. But in that moment the pending loss of her made me soft and frightened. I reached over and took her hand. "Stay safe," I said for the third time, as if I could charm the words.

"You, too." She took Lucienne's hand in her free hand. "Keep your mom safe."

"I will." She looked quite serious for a twelve-year-old, but then she had been a serious infant.

The threat of war intensified whatever we were to begin with. For Lucienne, it was being angry and serious and deeply thoughtful. I had become worried and flighty, forgetting things and sleeping badly. Keeping my emotions in check had become hard.

Juliette became brave.

Now, the threat bore down so hard my focus felt as sharp as a hawk's talon and I quivered with the need to flee. The border between Canada and us had never been defensive. It started as a quiet nod to neighbors who liked each other. It gained some teeth in the early terrorist years, and it still had those teeth. But there was nothing about that thin line between big countries that would stand up to a wall of robotic tanks or waves of battle drones.

Lucienne and I had our packs ready, locked in the trunk of the car. Everyone else who had stayed might have their cars loaded, too. Every moment we waited crawled up my nerves. I set my empty cup down. "Now."

Lucienne refused to look at me. She wanted to stay. She held her slender wrist up and touched her wristlet to Juliette's, her eyes staring at her as if she could change the world with the force of her gaze. "Stay connected. Promise?"

"Yes." Juliette's voice sounded thick with unsaid words. She leaned down and kissed us, Lucienne first and then me, on the forehead. Right after, she left, dropping her cups and ours in the bus bin just before she closed the back door quietly.

She had chosen to fight, picked a job as a sentinel and a relay, although I knew she had acquired a few knives and found unseen places to strap them. Pointless against a war of machinery. Half the city planned to fight.

I hadn't even bothered to hope she would see reason.

Maybe if we had been married or something, but we weren't, and Lucienne and I weren't hers to protect. But Lucienne was mine, and we were leaving.

Outside, the sky was the color of June, a tapestry in shades of gray, some parts light with sun and others pregnant with rain. Right after we climbed into the car and doors closed, Lucienne said, "I hate you."

"All twelve year olds hate their mothers."

"I hate you more than anyone."

"I know."

The car lurched forward. We settled into silence and devices, as if this were any trip to school or work in spite of the fact that emergency supplies and far too many pre-teen sized clothes filled every spot in the car that we didn't.

To my surprise the car was able to cross Lake Washington on the 520 bridge and catch side streets to interstate 90. National Guardsmen in bright orange vests with guns and knives waived cars forward and forward and forward again in spurts, letting new vehicles in from the side roads and the onramps in clumps and then letting the main group of us inch forward again. They appeared to be getting silent instructions from the same emergency traffic control that fed the cars, as if perhaps they were as extraneous as Juliette would surely be.

I packed and unpacked our packs, succeeding in making them feel bigger. Mostly, I berated myself for staying too long. My company had paid me a generous bonus to stay, Juliette had been a sort of bonus, and Lucienne had been working on a final project.

Besides, the Russians hadn't seemed real.

Lucienne alternated between glaring at me, fiddling with her wristlet, sleeping, and talking to her friends, most of whom had already left. Only two hid in Seattle: Lisa on a boat in Lake Union and Scott in a warehouse near the docks.

From time to time Lucienne narrated the news for me, and all of it seemed to be about numbers. Her voice came out flat and calm. "Forty thousand people have left the city this morning. All lanes of I5 southbound are stopped. Two northbound lanes have been opened for southbound traffic." A few moments later. "Thirty-two hundred people in Vancouver are reported dead."

While I gasped at that, Lucienne did not. She might as well have been playing a video game. "You know this is real?" I asked in spite of my better judgment.

She rolled her eyes.

Just after we crested the pass and started heading down toward Cle Elum, she gave a little gasp. "Juliette saw one. She sent me a picture."

The car braked and we swayed and then it started more slowly. I peered out, but there was nothing to see but lines of cars with dimmed lights and tall trees and stars. "Saw what?"

"A Russian tank. With robots. On the freeway. She sent me a picture."

"Can I see?"

She held her wrist up. The image had been taken at an odd angle, with a street light askew so it looked like it was about to fall down. The tank was light gray against a dark gray sky, all hard angles and sharp lines looming over the optically tilted light pole. It struck me hard, but I swallowed and squinted at it, trying not to be frightened. "I don't see the robot drivers."

"They don't look like people." She stared out the window, lying down so her view had to be mostly sky and the occasional tree. "We could walk faster than the car is going."

"We can't leave the car. We need it to sleep in."

"I don't want to live in the car."

I pointed a thumb at the mounds of stuff all around us. "Do you want to carry all this?"

She dug a piece of paper and a pencil out of her backpack, changed her seat so she sat up straighter, and started writing things down.

"Is that a list?"

"Hmmmhmmm." Her head bobbed up and down, her soft red curls catching a ray of afternoon sun. As usual, the weather had changed when we crossed the spine of the Cascades. Here, the sky was a dusty blue just darkening toward the gray-blue of dusk. The sun, behind us, would fall over the mountains soon.

"What is it a list of?"

"Everyone back home."

"We should start looking forward."

She practically snarled at me. "Isn't it bad enough that we left?"

I grit my teeth, clamping down on my anger. After I had taken enough breaths to feel back in control, I changed the subject. "Is the *Times* broadcasting anything?"

"Bellingham surrendered."

Such a strange phrase. It stuck in my heart, making me heavy with something deeper than fear. Dread? Bellingham was part-way between Vancouver and Seattle, a medium-sized town full of artists and tourists and expensive houses.

"There's fighting in Lynwood."

Even closer to Seattle. We had friends in Martha Lake, which was near Lynwood. But they had left three months ago, urging us to go. I had wanted to wait for Lucienne to get out of Junior High. Better to move between High Schools. I laughed, bitter. Better to pretend everything was fine. Until you couldn't any more.

The traffic in front of us stopped.

A woman in an orange vest rapped on the window.

I opened it a sliver, peering up at her. She was my age, or maybe older, with a grim smile. "Are you two okay?"

I nodded.

"Do you have food?"

Again, I nodded. Lucienne watched us quietly.

"Get off at the next exit."

"There's nothing there." I knew that. We needed to go one more exit to get to the stores or restaurants in Cle Elum. It was downhill. But I nodded, fully intending to ignore her.

"We're pulling everyone who is okay off the road to let babies and sick and the like have a head start. Take the opportunity to sleep." She rattled a can and an orange spot appeared on my windshield, some of the spray coming back to dust the edge of one of the other windows. "Hey!" I yelled at her.

She ignored me.

I watched her back, fuming. "We should have left a week ago."

"We shouldn't have left at all." She pointed at the other side of the highway. It had periodically filled with military trucks, but I hadn't seen any cars on it for hours. "We could go back home. That way is clear."

I'd read analysis that suggested if the Russians controlled Vancouver and Seattle they could run the whole Northwest. "We have to go east."

Lucienne glared at me again and went back to staring at her wristlet. Her anger filled the small car, washing against me, tempting me to rise to it and say something I'd regret later. I fought to stay silent, watching the sky roll by.

After a while she said, "Juliette is fighting. She has a gun. I didn't know she had a gun."

"How do you know?"

"We're friends. When her friends post a picture of her, I see it."

"What about your friends in Boulder?" That's where we were going. I had social media friends there. One had said he'd take us in for a few weeks. It was something. "Are they on your list?"

"They're not in any danger."

"Neither are we."

"That's the problem."

I sighed. It wasn't, not to me. Lucienne hadn't lost anyone close to her. Death was movies and a video games and books, but it wasn't real.

She pointed up. "Planes."

"Maybe you shouldn't look at pictures of Juliette. Not if she's fighting." Did I have to tell Lucienne she might see Juliette die? Did I have to spell out as if she were two?

"The planes are going into Seattle."

"What direction are they flying?"

"They're coming from the south."

So they had to be ours. The lines of cars started moving again. A blond teen girl in an orange vest made everyone with orange paint on their cars get off the highway. We were in an abandoned ski area lot, the pavement overgrown with weeds but serviceable enough. The car followed directions, and parked us in a mob, with just enough room between cars for doors to open. It felt like concert parking. The concert of war, maybe.

We slid out of the car and followed the pointing finger of an old woman with shocking green-gold eyes who said, "Don't leave your car for more than an hour. Be back in your car before first light. We don't guarantee your safety or anyone else's, anything you have could get stolen." It sounded like a chore for her to say all those things, like she'd repeated it so often she was running out of voice.

"Is there a bathroom?" I asked.

"Latrine—that way. Bring a light."

"A light?" But I did. I understood after we waited until after dark for our turn. All around, men peed in bushes. We might have if they weren't doing it, but when one of the women in front of use went off to the bushes, Lucienne and I glanced at each other and shook our heads. Two days ago I had sat in front of a computer screen helping people who wanted to have their dogs walked while they were at work. The deluded helping the deluded, the last ones out of Seattle except the fighters.

Some people in the line talked to each other but we didn't. Lucienne stood and stared at her wristlet and I poked at mine from time to time, but I was not good with it. Not really. I could get the headlines but not read the stories.

The latrine stank so badly we walked away fast after we used it. We huddled in the car in the dark, packs for pillows, jackets for blankets. Even after the seats folded themselves away there wasn't much room. We ate food bars and nuts. Lucienne let out a small squeak and then said, "Mom?"

"Yes?"

"Lisa's boat just blew up."

I closed my eyes, seeing a girl just Lucienne's age, with dark hair and eyes and a propensity for wearing yellow. She'd come to our house for dinner once. Last year. "Is she okay?"

"She's running through the streets. There's no one with her. I don't see anyone, anyway. All I have is her stream and her track."

That would be a live stream of shots taken every few seconds and discarded, and a bunch of orange points that looked like video game trails showing where Lisa was and had been. She would have it; they were friends. I wouldn't.

I hadn't even location-friended Juliette. I didn't want to see her die.

Lucienne, her eyes fixed and wide, watched Lisa run for her life, staring at a screen that was two inches wide and one inch high. Her lips were a thin line. Her pinky shook so hard it made her screen quiver. She grabbed her hand with her other hand and stilled it.

I wanted to hold her. She'd stopped even letting me touch her a year ago.

I whispered. "Is Lisa still okay?"

She nodded.

I watched her, afraid for her friends, afraid for her. In what world was the United States attacked?

"Her light stopped."

"Maybe she's catching her breath."

Lucienne shook her wrist. "Maybe she ran out of battery."

"I hope so, honey."

"We should be there." She turned away from me, staring at the wall, and after a while her breath stilled into sleep.

Even though they were bulletproof, the windows were made to hear things through. An owl hooted somewhere outside and two men talked nearby, their words too thin for me to make out meaning. I wanted to stay awake, but I had barely slept the night before, and I drifted off into strange dreams.

I woke to find Lucienne gone.

No note. No nothing. One of the packs was gone as well.

The car had grown cold. "Car," I commanded it, "Let me out."

I checked my wristlet. I had location-friended my daughter. Clearly she had blocked me.

I raced through the cars toward the latrine, watching for her. She wasn't in line. I ducked under a tree, peed, and went back the other way. I had a flashlight in my pocket, but no coat, no pack. I went back and gathered those things, left her a note that I'd gone to find her. Told her I'd return to the car in an hour.

Surely she couldn't walk to Seattle.

More cars drove in along the long road, passing us, going who knew how far. Everywhere that I saw people out and about, standing between cars and talking, I asked after Lucienne. "Have you seen a twelve-year-old? Red hair. Black shirt. A little skinny?"

They all shook their heads.

Three men agreed to help me, and then a woman. Soon there were ten or more people fanned out in the dark, calling her name.

My breath was fast and hard, my heart racing. I thought about texting Juliette, but surely he had other things on his mind.

The hour passed, with nothing. My helpers agreed to keep looking and I made my way back to our parking place, eyeing the barely lightening sky. We were supposed to be ready at dawn.

She wasn't back there. I added to my note, and then found I couldn't get up. I didn't have the strength. Tears fell onto my hands.

Maybe she was texting Juliette. I texted her. <Lucienne missing> <Have U heard from her?>

God, I sounded cold. No intro. Just the fact's ma'am. I added <how are you?>

Nothing. I used my arms to force myself up, and started looking again, glancing at my wrist from time to time.

Light started to spill over the horizon in earnest. Birds sang.

I hadn't seen my daughter for six hours. When did she leave? Where was she?

What could I have said differently?

Was she safe?

I found a thin, stooped man wearing the ubiquitous orange vest. "Have you seen a child?"

"How old?"

"Twelve."

"Do you have a picture?"

"Of course." I sent him one. He futzed with his wristlet, then looked up and said. "Go back to your car."

"I'm not leaving her."

He spoke slowly, as if I were hard of hearing. "You need to be in your car for it to get out of the lot."

"Other cars can go around it."

"Go to your car. We'll find you."

"Okay." But I didn't. I started jogging between rows of cars, watching people wake up. People in orange started yelling at everyone to get in their cars, and I waved at them. Sure. Sure. I was going.

Where was she?

Engines began to turn on.

Cars pulled out, a slow, depressing line. Our still and silent car probably slowed them down some, but I couldn't tell.

A drone flew over. News drone? Battle drone?

As the cars near me started, lights flipping on and soft engine noise declaring life, I jogged between them, heading for the front of the lot, suddenly afraid she'd been imprisoned in someone's car. I wanted to watch all the cars leave and be sure Lucienne wasn't trapped in any of them.

Another drone came. They dipped and dove, and shot at nothing and no one shot at them. But people everywhere watched them, sitting up straight and leaning out windows and taking pictures with wrists and other small cameras. The drones were eerily silent, as were the cars, everything so electric and quiet the sound of birds singing came through the morning clearly.

A hand landed on my shoulder when I wasn't expecting it and I jumped. A tall man in an orange vest striped with safety yellow. His sunglasses—pushed on top of his head—matched. I hadn't seen such a full beard in years, brown but starting to grow in gray. "Go to your car."

"I have to find my daughter."

"They found her."

"Who?"

"A friend. Up the road. In a tow truck. He's bringing her back."

"Up the road? Where?"

"She was on her way to Seattle. You'd have never caught her. She was almost at the crest." His look was disapproving, as if I'd lost her on purpose.

Shame and anger and relief all warred inside me but I just said, "Thank you."

"Wait in your car."

I didn't feel like being compliant, but I compromised by heading toward the car and then hovering within a few thousand feet of it.

Juliette didn't text me back. I tried not to think about that, but it was like not thinking about pink elephants. I kept imagining her falling.

Lucienne hadn't turned on her location beacons, so I couldn't tell how long it would take for her to get back to me. I fought for calm. I had to be calm. I could keep her safe if I could stay calm.

The lot was almost empty, even the drones gone. A bald eagle rode a thermal above the lot. I periodically read headlines. Fighting everywhere in Seattle. People were fleeing from Tacoma and a truck had taken down a bridge, snarling traffic. The Russians were starting down two more border points, one in Montana and one in North Dakota. They hadn't yet captured anything in Eastern Canada, and our troops were helping the Canadians as well as fighting for us. People were rushing to join, and I thought of Juliette again, and wondered where she was. Almost everyone else I knew had left Seattle before we did.

When the bearded man brought Lucienne back, her face was so white I wondered what he had said to her, and my anger fled into some other protective state. "Are you okay?" I asked as soon as he had gone.

She swallowed. "Lisa's dead."

"Do you know that?"

She stared at the ground and mumbled. "Someone else is using her wristlet. Someone who speaks another language."

"Is that all you know?"

"Yes."

"Is that why you left?"

She toed the ground. "I wanted to help her."

There was still a chasm between us. I could feel it, and I made myself stand still and not reach for her no matter how much I wanted to. "I'm sorry."

"I haven't heard from Juliette. I don't know if she's okay, either."

"I texted her when you were missing."

"I don't want to leave home," she said. "I can't help anyone from here. I can't do anything useful." Her voice started to rise. "I can't be a hero."

Was that what this was about? "Of course you can. Give it a little time."

"I want to be a hero now." She was almost shouting, my little serious child who almost always followed directions.

My voice rose in return, matching hers, rising above it. "Like what? A comic book hero?"

She simply stared at me, as if the question had shocked her still.

I stepped toward her. "Is Lisa a hero?"

Silence.

Anger licked through my bones, burning away any self-control I had left. "Does dying make you a hero? We could arrange that." I sounded snappy, even to myself. Mean. Horrible. Noisy. I can only imagine what I sounded like to her. "We are family. We need to keep each other alive. There will be more chance to die in your life. You'll have them. Plenty of them. But you have to learn more before you can be a hero." I took a deep heaving breath.

Lucienne eyes widened. I never yelled.

Except now. I kept my voice high, piling my fear for her into it. "Lisa is no hero. She's just dead. Or not. You don't know. But if she dies, it didn't do any good. Death doesn't do anyone any good."

Lucienne said nothing, merely stared.

"It's true. You can choose to die any day. Any day. But you can also choose to live. We're going to live."

"I want to fight."

"You have to live to fight!"

My wrist buzzed, interrupted my tirade. Juliette. <Did you find her?>

I felt parts of me relax, breathe out. <Yes>

<I'm OK. Sleeping now. Text you tomorrow. Keep her safe.>

This time all I felt was relief. No warring emotions. Just relief. I showed Lucienne the texts. "She's fighting to keep you and I safe. We should go."

A tear streaked down her face.

I couldn't help myself. I reached a hand out and plucked it from her cheek.

She stepped into me for the first time in two years, and her arms curled around me.

"I love you," I whispered. "I need for you to be safe."

"I never hated you."

My whole body shook. "I know."

If the Censors betray us, run for the border. I will know you've gone, and that will set me free, too. At that point they'll be no better than the Shadows. Run, and wait for me.

Joyce Reynolds-Ward

The Notice

JOYCE REYNOLDS-WARD

FOR ONCE IT WASN'T DARK AND RAINING WHEN SHE LEFT WORK. Yarrow hesitated in the lobby of the medical office building where she worked, surveying the outdoors as she adjusted her coat. There was the slightest hint of gold light to the west that reflected into the street from an upper row of windows on the skyscraper opposite her building. Her fingers itched to seize the warm golden glow and spin it into a bright web to cheer those around her. It was one thing she had done to make Jenny smile even in the darkest political hours.

No, she told herself. Yarrow knew better than to try to weave the light, even to bring joy to others and divert their thoughts from the Shadow War's necessity. Doing so might trigger her building's wards—more than that, the secret Witches Resistance Council had advised those like Yarrow to hide their presence outside of work. *Lie low. Avoid drawing attention from the Censors. Fear of the Shadows has spilled into fear of all magic, even for good. Don't risk yourself without good cause!*

Unfortunately, bringing pleasant thoughts to the non-witches around her didn't fall in the category of "good cause." Still, Yarrow leaned against the floor-to-ceiling window and gazed at the golden light before it faded, to hearten herself at the least. She savored the glow's cheery warmth, delaying the moment when she would have to pass through the building's wards. She could remember Jenny's smile. Maybe she could see this quick glow even in Relocation Camp #5. Thinking about Jenny helped Yarrow ignore the handful of people who glowered at her.

Witch. Outsider. Their emotions were so palpable that Yarrow almost expected to see a second being embodying that fear and anger stalking alongside those who glared at her. The Council was right, but oh, she wished for the days before the Censors and the Shadows had engaged in this war, when witches like her were honored rather than hated and feared.

Who knows what witches are safe? Best put them all in a camp, she picked up from one man who glared the hardest at her. Yarrow also caught a glimpse of his memory of a beloved woman melting away as one of the alien Shadow fell over her. She shuddered. Even though she also sensed one of the protective charms of her making to keep his emotions from bleeding out and calling to the Shadows, he still projected hard. A recent loss.

But he still hated her, like so many of those who benefited from her healing and her charms, even though the bracelets on her wrists restrained her and bled magic from her. The curse of the Shadows that hung over the City meant that memories of the good things that witches did faded more quickly than the destructive moments. People only remembered was that the Censors had declared all witches, all magic, to be dangerous, whether positive or destructive, even as they used it.

In cynical moments Yarrow let herself wonder if there really was a difference between the Censors and the Shadows. Before Jenny's capture, she would have persuaded Yarrow out of those moments. Now, Yarrow wasn't so sure.

She shook herself. Of course there was a difference. Yarrow heaved a sigh as the last of the golden light faded, regretting that she had allowed politics to distract her from savoring the glow. She tapped the bracelets that controlled her magic to the outside non-work setting, and winced as a dull pressure rose in her sinuses. The world about her darkened. Not as bad as it would be without that fleeting memory of sunglow.

Don't think about the Censors, she told herself. *Think about home.* Maybe the bus ride would be peaceful and she would have the energy to tell small stories to Carlos and Marisol, Leslie and Maria's kids. It had been a slow magic day at work, no healing required of her so she had made her charms all day. That might leave enough magic in her daily allotment to illustrate her stories with the animated creatures the kids loved.

But first she had to get home without incident. Yarrow steeled herself and went through the doorway. Cold fire lanced through her bracelets, vibrating through her wrists as the building's daemon questioned the data chip in the bracelets. Sensing no wrongdoing from Yarrow for her day's work, the sharpness of the cold fire faded as she passed through the vestibule and the second door. Still, the dull throb in her forehead grew stronger as she went outside. This query from the building had hurt more than usual, and the cold wind whispering through the skyscraper canyons didn't help.

Once she reached the bus shelter, Yarrow stood in the yellow-painted rectangle on the pavement outside the shelter labeled WITCHES ONLY. No one came near her. Two schoolboys hissed mockingly at her in low whispers; she ignored them, knowing the tone too well to make the effort to make sense of the hurtful words. She huddled down into her coat as the damp cold wind whipped around her, relieved when the bus finally pulled up.

The line to get on the bus stretched almost to her rectangle. Yarrow waited as the normals loaded, worrying. The next bus might not reach her stop before curfew, and she'd have to use magic to hide herself and get home safely. But at last the back door of the bus opened. She slid in and found her customary seat on the steps, next to another woman with witch's restraint bracelets and the witch glyph on her coat. They sat together gingerly, careful not to touch in case their bracelets objected to the contact.

The bus stopped. Yarrow and the other witch stood and pressed against opposite sides of the stairwell as the norms left. One man banged his bag against Yarrow's shins. She bit her lip to keep from giving him the satisfaction of knowing he had caused her pain. He scowled at her.

"—witches," she heard him say as she sank into herself again on her stairwell perch. At least she hadn't heard the epithet clearly. Yarrow leaned her head against the stairwell wall and whispered a tiny obscure charm to make her less noticeable. Her bracelets vibrated a warning, sending sharp tingles up and down her arms. Yarrow closed her eyes and breathed through her mouth. A little more pain and a little less magic was tolerable compared to the possibility of *just one more* encounter like that.

She'd be home soon. Safe for another night. She hoped.

And it was still another night without Jenny. Another night when she wished that Jenny had taken the bracelets—but the Jenny who would do that was not the woman Yarrow loved.

One of us has to stay safe for the future of our kind, Jenny had said. *You have more to contribute with your charms and healing magic. All I know how to do is fight—*she had shrugged here*—and I can't do much against the Shadows with my skills. I'm an organizer. But the Censors won't let me stay free for long— if I know you are safe, then I can stay strong and organize the Resistance against both Censors and Shadows, even in a Relocation Camp.*

Yarrow swallowed hard. Sometimes she wondered if Jenny was doing more good in Relocation Camp #5 than she would have done as a tame organizer for the Censors.

The streetlight at her stop had burned out again. Yarrow tensed as she stepped off of the bus, switching from *obscure* to a *scan* charm of equal strength. Sometimes the Censors switched off the light to let anti-witch mobs hunt freely. Prickles of pain radiated from her bracelets as they protested the stronger charm. She scanned behind the low brick wall dividing the patio of a condominium complex from the sidewalk, the most likely space for an ambusher to hide. Nothing. She extended her scan to include the low row of arborvitae lining the foundation of the apartments next to the condos. Nothing. Perhaps the light had legitimately burned out.

Nonetheless, Yarrow remained cautious as she walked two blocks past increasingly shabby apartment buildings until she reached the rundown two-story complex that held her studio. The light being out could also mean that a raid was imminent. But no dangers lurked in the narrow dark courtyard between the two wings of the building.

The main entry door was ajar so that she didn't need to punch her code to get in, a thin thread of light spilling into the

dark outside. Not right. Yarrow pushed it open, alert. Still, there
was nothing worrisome in the dingy foyer. Yet.

She climbed the stairs, the silence adding to her worry. Far
too quiet. No mouth-watering scent of spicy dinner wafting from
Abdul and Kareen's apartment down the north wing hallway on
the main floor. No kid noise from Maria and Leslie's apartment
near the second floor landing. No distant mumbles of TVs from
other apartments as she walked to her door. It was as if no one
else was at home. Everyone else should be in the building now,
comfy and cozy against a world turned alien.

Dread clutched at Yarrow's stomach. *Has something
happened to Jenny?* Her limited freedom had been the deal
Jenny had made with the Censors to go peacefully to the Camp
without provoking a battle that would only benefit the Shadows.

A yellow sheet of paper on her door heightened her sense of
doom. Yarrow detached it with shaking hands. The words
splayed across the narrow paper in an incongruously cheerful
magenta font.

RELOCATION ORDER
24 HOUR NOTICE.
DO NOT GO TO WORK.
DO NOT LEAVE THE BUILDING
UNTIL NATIONAL SECURITY COMES FOR YOU.
DO NOT WORK MAGIC.
BE PACKED.
NO MORE THAN TWO BAGS.

Yarrow gulped. She crumpled the notice into a tight ball in
one hand and unlocked her door, her hands shaking even
though she felt a faint twinge of magic in the notice. She
slammed the door shut behind her. Then she spotted an
envelope on the floor close to the door, her name inscribed on it
in fine black calligraphy. *Now what?* She reluctantly picked it
up. The envelope was of good quality, the type used for fancy
invitations or thank yous. Her heart started to pound harder.
Could it be—? The Resistance Council used cards like this to
communicate. It was easier to authenticate physical cards, and
the Censors couldn't monitor them as well as they could elec-
tronic communications.

Yarrow lightly tapped the bright red seal on the back flap. A faint chime sounded. Authentic. A missive from the Resistance Council. Hands shaking, Yarrow broke the seal and took out the card.

DESTROY AFTER READING flashed at the top in bright red letters.

Underneath, in the same fine calligraphy that had been on the envelope, the message continued.

Time is of the essence and the Censors are watching the building. Raid hit at 2 pm today. Got everyone but me, Maria, and the kids. Abdul is dead for certain. We need to free the survivors and your services are required by the Council. Censors mean to manipulate Jenny and discredit her work in the Camp by making a big deal about capturing you, claim you're working with the Shadows. Get your things ready and wait for my knock. Destroy this now. "Burn to nothingness."
Leslie
RC-authenticated

"Burn to nothingness," Yarrow repeated the auto-destruct command, staring at the missive as both card and envelope disappeared in a bright flash. Her bracelets jolted sharply but she didn't notice the pain. Leslie? *Leslie* was the Resistance Council lead in the building? Chunky little Leslie with her bright grin? Then again, Leslie was active, with a muscular core that meant she instead of Maria was the one doing their family's share of the heavy work around the apartment complex.

Yarrow reached into the armoire that held her big emergency backpack. Inside the pack was the bag filled with her magical implements and other things she might want should she need to flee in a hurry. She had hoped never to need it, knew it was futile should the Censors decide to bring her in when she was at work, but still kept it ready just in case. After all, the Resistance Council hadn't called upon her to do anything more than her daily job since the Censors had imprisoned Jenny. They had decided that the work she did making protective charms for the war effort against the Shadows was a higher priority for her small talents than working more openly for the Resistance like Jenny did. Yarrow had turned in enough of her personal magical supplies to quell any suspicions that the Censors might have that she was anything other than a submissive, docile witch who would do what they ordered. Even if her girlfriend was Jenny, face of the Resistance to both Censors and Shadows. That agreement Jenny had made was supposed to keep Yarrow safe.

But what if the Censors had decided to default on their agreement? War news had not been good. Unfortunately Leslie's note rang too true. Yarrow had not knowingly done anything to aid the Shadows—now she was glad she *hadn't* woven that golden glow this afternoon. Innocent as that action might have seemed at the time, it still could have been construed as a signal to the Shadows.

Anything could be a signal to the Shadows, she reminded herself. And she was wasting time brooding. She turned back to her pack, and pulled the gold-colored leather bag that held her magic supplies out of it. She eased the bag's ties and began her inventory. Her small charms—still potent. The potion vials were full in their stiff leather case, none of the seals broken. Yarrow slipped two ring charms onto her fingers, uncertain why except that they called to her. One ring held a small vial of consecrated salt. Her athame tingled as she brushed her fingers against its black hilt and the moonstone sigil set within it. She placed it to one side, planning to hang it from her belt once she changed clothing.

Lastly, she pulled out the small velveteen jewelry bag and shook out its contents. The silver wire-wrapped amethyst on a silver chain slid into her hand, her bracelets stinging as the amethyst began to glow. Her power token, the original and real one. She had turned a carefully synthesized fake into the Censors—an action that if discovered would land her in a Relocation Camp.

Maybe that was another reason they were taking her in now.

But why warn me like this? Why not just grab me on the street? Better publicity? If they knew that token was a fake, they wouldn't play with me like this. They would know I was strong enough to hide myself even with the bracelets.

They didn't know she had her true token. The Censors wanted her afraid and weak, the better to break her will and strengthen their power.

I won't let that happen. Yarrow shuddered and closed her hand into a fist around the amethyst, embracing the pain from the bracelets instead of rejecting it. Then she hung the amethyst around her neck, ignoring the persistent complaining prickle from her bracelets. She drew a deep, shuddering breath as the amethyst settled between her breasts, already feeling stronger.

I will be docile no longer, she vowed. Until she heard otherwise, she now had to assume that Jenny's agreement with the Censors was null and void. *I am free to be myself!*

Yarrow quickly changed into jeans. She strapped the sheathed athame on her heavy leather belt, then filled the backpack with the rest of the things she needed to flee.

That done, Yarrow straightened up and looked around the studio. This tiny studio had been home for six months, third place in less than two years. She paused to finger the three porcelain horses she had managed to bring along until now, all gifts from Jenny. This time she would have to leave them.

Tap-tap. Tap-tap-TAP-tap rattled on the door as she finished tying the laces on her hiking boots.

Friend or foe? she queried the amethyst, reaching up with her left hand to clutch it through the wool sweater.

It pulsed warm in her hand. *Friend.*

Yarrow dropped her hand and peered through the spyhole. Leslie stood in front of the door, looking around nervously. Yarrow let her in.

"I'm ready," Yarrow said.

"Good," Leslie gulped. "We have to go. Now. They got Maria and the kids, too!"

Chills gripped Yarrow's gut. "But the kids aren't witches!"

"They're tainted by witch contact," Leslie shook her head and moaned. "Come on! Let's go!"

Yarrow bent to grab her backpack, something about the tone in Leslie's voice setting her on edge. Plus it just didn't sound right. Coolness radiated from the amethyst, confirming her reaction. *Something not right.*

"I have to check something," she said to Leslie, kneeling next to her backpack, using it to cover her movements as she unsheathed her athame.

The *not-right* feeling grew.

"Hurry up! What could be so important?" Leslie knelt next to Yarrow and the *not-right* sensation became stronger. *But the amethyst said she was safe—no, it said she was a friend. Not that she was safe.*

Yarrow looked into Leslie's eyes.

"What happened with Maria and the kids?" she asked calmly, reaching up to grasp her amethyst with her left hand as she held the athame hidden.

Friend but not safe came back to her.

"Why are you wasting time?" Leslie grabbed and shook Yarrow. Yarrow dropped the amethyst and twisted Leslie's right hand behind her back.

"*What happened with Maria and the kids?*" she demanded, touching the point of the athame to the jugular vein in Leslie's neck.

"Why are you wasting our time with this?" Leslie's voice quavered and for the first time Yarrow noticed that Leslie's bracelets were gone. But there was no flow of power from Leslie like there should be from a witch with no bracelets. *Why didn't I notice that right away? I should have—unless—*

Rumors held that the Censors sometimes produced bracelets that created rather than restricted magic, calling upon the City's shared magical protections to empower a non-witch. Those same rumors said there was no way to tell the difference until the bracelets were gone. Yarrow had never knowingly encountered someone wearing those reversed bracelets. Was Leslie to be the first?

Leslie always pooh-poohed those stories, she remembered.

"What happened to your bracelets?" Yarrow asked, even as the pain radiating from her own bracelets grew stronger. "Why are you in such a hurry?"

Leslie wouldn't meet Yarrow's eyes. "We've got to go. Now!"

Yarrow pressed harder on Leslie's neck. The athame stirred in her hand and nicked Leslie's vein. A bead of blood welled up, then disappeared, sucked up by the athame.

"You betrayed Abdul and the others, didn't you?" Yarrow asked. "You're a spy for the Censors!"

"I—I—I didn't mean to!" Leslie stammered. Her eyes widened. "We've got to go! Fast!"

"Why? So you can hand me over to the Censors?" Yarrow delicately drew the point down Leslie's neck, steeling herself for the next move. If Leslie truly was a traitor to the Witches Council—*Traitor's blood will set you free,* Jenny had told her.

"Don't. For the love of all that is sacred, *don't,*" Leslie choked, finally now meeting Yarrow's eyes. "If I bring you then they'll let Maria and the kids go."

Don't drink, Yarrow commanded her athame. She scraped some of the trickling blood from Leslie's neck with the athame's edge. She brushed the blood onto both bracelets, then opened the cap on the salt ring, sprinkling the content over the bracelets.

"Unbind," she whispered.

She didn't know whether to be disappointed or elated when the bracelets fell off.

Leslie crumpled up, burying her face in her hands. "I didn't want to do it, Yarrow. But they threatened Maria and the kids if we didn't spy on everyone here. Especially you."

"But you did." The flood of regained power was almost intoxicating, begging her to use magic to coerce Leslie to *explain,* but Yarrow pushed it back.

Leslie darted toward the door and Yarrow grabbed her arm again, yanking her back.

"Ow!" Leslie struggled until Yarrow held the athame to her neck. "Yarrow, by all that is holy, please— for Maria, and the children, *please.*"

"Why should I trust you?" Yarrow hissed.

"You don't understand," Leslie protested. "I was just trying to save Maria and the kids."

The athame's hilt didn't change temperature. So a half-truth.

"Where were you taking me?"

Leslie sniffled. Yarrow pressed harder with the athame.

"The North Square!" Leslie finally screamed.

The North Square, where witches were publicly humiliated and tortured to force their submission to the Censors for the Shadow War. Jenny had explicitly bargained to avoid that fate for

Yarrow, and she'd done her best to be properly submissive so she wouldn't be taken to the Square.

This means Jenny's agreement is broken. I can't stay in the City. She fingered her other ring. It should be able to guide her to a safe place for tonight.

But first she had to deal with Leslie. Yarrow swallowed hard, then drew on her now freed magic.

"Hold," she breathed. Leslie gulped for air and strained to rise as Yarrow got up but could do no more than flex against invisible restraints. Yarrow picked up her discarded bracelets, studying them. She fished out a couple of twist-ties from the bottom of the backpack, then wove the twist-ties between the two bracelets. Next, she ran her fingers along them, whispering the charm she had used to make bindings against the Shadows for the War's sake. The ties swelled into a solid chain linking the bracelets.

Yarrow fastened Leslie's wrists behind her back. Then she used an extra blouse and another binding charm to create a second restraint on Leslie's ankles.

"Forget I was ever here," she commanded the studio and Leslie, activating the last charm Jenny had left her. Then she tiptoed down the hallway to the stairs. Instead of going out the front, Yarrow continued to the basement. She raised a shade to hide herself, and let herself out the back door, hesitating before climbing up the outside stairwell, remembering what Jenny had told her as she thought about where to go now.

If the Censors betray us, run for the border. I will know you've gone, and that will set me free, too. At that point they'll be no better than the Shadows. Run, and wait for me.

Yarrow wrapped her hand around the amethyst again.

I am free, Jenny.

The stone warmed in her hand. *Run free. Run free and testify to what we endure now. I will do what I can.*

I will, she promised. Then she headed down the alleyway.

She had to find a place for tonight. Then tomorrow, early, before her absence was discovered, she'd slip down to the river to join other wanderers. Drift with them to the frontier, hiding her magic until she had the chance to cross the border—and hope that the curse of the Shadows and Censors had not spread further, had not eliminated the belief in hope. In magic that created rather than destroyed. In joy rather than fear.

She hoped her plan would work.

It had to work, for all their sakes.

Eyes forward, head down, focus on the task of the day—
same task as every day from here on in: Stop the visitors,
put 'em down, send 'em back.
Randee Dawn

Can't Find My Way Home

RANDEE DAWN

"GRAB HIM, GARCIA!"

The creature whizzes by so fast it's like he has lightning feet, and knowing these punks he just might.

Instinctively Emissary Sergeant Tony Garcia lashes out with one hand, but the strap of his XL-PEP hurls the weapon over his shoulder and throws him off-balance, so his fingers just graze the runner's arm.

Go with it, he thinks and leans into the twist, thrusting his body forward so he can bash the creature from the other side. It's like running into a brick wall, but the runner tumbles into the torn-up fallow field and Garcia shifts the Peppie back into position.

"*Fan nóiméad –*" the creature raises its hand.

Garcia squeezes the trigger, the concussive pulse rocking him back. He recovers and prepares to mash his muddy boot into the creature's chest, but there's no need. The thing—looks male, but who the hell knows for sure—rolls on its side and vomits reddish-purple fluid into the wrecked grass, then starts shaking. All of its clothing, if that's what you can call it, starts to disintegrate. The EMP pulse doesn't hurt it, but it nullifies whatever sick crap these things carry over when they cross. Garcia guesses it's like a human taking a two-by-four to the back of the head.

Clap. Clap. Emissary Lieutenant Matt Wainwright, Garcia's patrol buddy, stands to one side and lowers his hands. "Will you do 'Swan Lake' next time?"

Wainwright's a prick, but he's in charge and this is Garcia's first day in the field since the incident, so he doesn't rise to the challenge. Eyes forward, head down, focus on the task of the day—same task as every day from here on in: Stop the visitors, put 'em down, send 'em back when possible. When not possible, there's always the plasma setting on the PEP. After that, the pits.

Though on that last one, Garcia only knows secondhand. The pits are new to him. New to everyone.

"Got my stripes for grace and style," he growls and crouches alongside the prostrate thing on the ground. Not porcelain; those ones tend not to run. They just lob spells and Lord help you if you're in those crosshairs. Garcia's seen more than one unlucky soldier that ended up half out of his skull, strapped down in the field mobile hospital unit.

Nah, this one's a shifter with skin that changes shades depending on mood. Right now it's going from the color of its own puke to a dark green and back to pale brown. Shifters are less trouble, generally speaking. Worst they do is make it downpour on you or send a swarm of bees your way. Attacks in tune with nature, like. Garcia takes a small sniff; the creature should smell like upchuck and sweat and terror—but nope. What Garcia gets in his nostrils right now is fresh-mown grass on a sunny day....

"You gonna ask him on a date or get him on his feet?"

Wainwright again. Garcia shakes his head; for a minute there, he was back home in Tennessee. Almost heard the dog barking. Craziest thing. "Shit," he says, standing. "These things mess with your head."

"You'd know," says Wainwright, tossing him a blanket. "Wrap it up and get its hands tight."

Garcia restrains a desire to flip him the bird and glances back down. The shaking's stopped but now the creature is buck naked. When the EMP from the weapon hits them it knocks all the special out at once, and that means every stitch of the fey creatures' clothing—whether it's fine silk linen or stitched-together bark—dissolves into nothing. Like it isn't even real. Maybe the creatures aren't even real. Maybe the Peacekeepers have been fighting ghosts all this time.

He toes the creature—a young one, practically a kid. Except probably older than Garcia by a couple hundred years. *They look like us*, the instructors coached. *They sound like us. But they are not people. Do not name them. Use the number system.*

One bright green eye flies open, then the second. The kid's mouth curls back but he doesn't bare teeth. "Up," says Garcia, waving, and slowly the creature comes to its feet. Yep, male. Can be hard to tell with these ones—all dressed up most of 'em can go either way, but without a stitch on this is clearly a dude. He stands, arms crossed and bare-assed to the French countryside, not even attempting to cover himself like any respectable human would.

"D78," says Wainwright, stepping in and giving the kid his designation. "That's you."

The kid doesn't blink.

"I know you understand me," he continues, and pokes the kid once in the shoulder for emphasis. "Just want you to know that if you do anything other than follow orders, these little tools have another setting."

Garcia hefts his XL. Some call them PEPs—Pulsed Energy Projectiles—some Peppies. It's all the same to him; you shoot the runners with the pulse to slow 'em up and protect yourself from spells, then if they don't cooperate you switch to plasma. They'll burn, same as humans. And while they do heal pretty freaking fast, no creature has been shown to grow back a seared-off limb.

"Get him dressed," says Wainwright. "Don't feel like seeing fairy dick waving in the breeze, if you know what I mean."

"Feeling inadequate?" asks Garcia, reaching into his pack and withdrawing a blanket and rope. He hands both to the kid, gesturing that he should cover himself with the blanket and use the rope as a belt. He notices that the creature—the kid—has no navel. Another freakishness. Maybe it was there once, and healed up. He'll never know.

"Right," says Wainwright. "We're on the move. Get the hands tied."

Garcia shrugs. "Can if you want, but he's not doing anything but walking 'til that pulse wears off."

"Your choice," he says. "Back to base. Hup hup."

They turn and head south, away from the coastline. Behind them, the place where the air had been shimmering falls still again.

Finding D78 means they'll head back to camp, and it comes as a relief to Garcia after a long morning with Wainwright's eyes crawling on him like giant insects. Shipping two officers out together is no accident; Garcia knows he's on indefinite probation since the incident. But now that they have a creature in custody the mission has changed. When possible, they used to send 'em home, now they drag 'em back to camp. Once this one is processed they can grab hot lunch from the mess instead of having to hoover down another MRE or cardboard protein bar in the field.

Wainwright and Garcia are just one of twelve patrols that make up this local division of the United Nations Peacekeeper Force, an international group of soldiers stationed a few miles inland off the coast of northern France. Why France? Garcia has no clue, except that it's close to the QZ—quarantine zone. Lately the teams have been showing up with three or four of the creatures every couple of hours. Depending on what time you return to camp with your capture you can count on about an hour turnaround to eat and rest, then it's back out again.

It was Garcia who spotted the shimmer hanging in the air while out with Wainwright that morning—the guys like to call it an airhole, which is easier and crasser than saying what it really is: a portal between the real world and some other dimension where, apparently, actual mythical fairies live. Nobody spots airholes like Garcia does—he's always been No. 1 in the platoon for that, which is why they only kept him desked as long as was minimally necessary.

The portals are what the creatures keep slipping through, these random shimmers that cough out completely unwelcome visitors ready to make magic. Or trouble. Or both. The portal isn't open to humans though, far as Garcia knows—he never heard of anyone slipping through. 'Course, the locals inside the QZ on the other side of the English Channel claim to have gone back and forth for centuries, but that's what's called a fairy tale and nobody believes that shit.

Except Garcia has seen the "other side"—for about thirty seconds, and that's where his trouble began. About ten weeks ago, while out with a larger patrol, he spotted a working portal and no visitors in sight. Peering inside, he froze in place at the sight of *her* while the scent of fresh-baked bread with rosemary wafted through the portal. She *spoke* to him. Then the shimmer closed up and he was left standing, alone and hungry, when the rest of his squad jogged up and asked why the hell he was talking to the air.

Explanations got laughs. Insistence on his story got people worried, and landed him in a long debriefing. Maybe they believed him, maybe they didn't. Either way, Garcia was yanked out of the field and slammed behind a desk writing press releases while having twice-daily convos with Peacekeeper shrinks and intel officers. When he realized no one was paying attention to what he was telling them, he shifted gears and told them what they wanted to hear: that it was a hallucination. So they sent him back to his unit. But the whole experience was humiliating for a field soldier, and worse—the black mark on his record meant he might never rise in rank again.

So earlier this morning when he spotted the airhole with Wainwright, he didn't go near—just pointed. "Over there," he told the Lieutenant. "Two o'clock."

Wainwright turned around but before he'd even stopped moving the creature came through the hole like he was folding himself through a crack in reality. He stumbled to the ground, bumped into a fence pole, spotted Wainwright and Garcia and took off. Or tried to.

D78 was clearly a solo, but usually more came through at a time. They emerged in clumps of four, six and even twelve, stumbling out and gazing around for a second before they just began walking. Originally, patrols were told to follow discreetly at a distance, to see if visitors would lead to houses where they'd be given sanctuary, but in the end it seemed that the fey who came over had no plans at all. They walked, and when they found clothes hanging on a line they stole them and dressed like natives to blend in.

But until they did that they were easy to track: wherever bare fey feet touched earth the grass sprouted wild, sometimes with little patches of bluebells and primroses to boot. It was something that went unnoticed in June, July, August. Not in March. Their footprints—at least until they could purloin some human shoes—were small and green and smelled of pastries.

D78 says nothing. He has no expression, no recognition that it's probably only a couple degrees above freezing and all he's wearing is a blanket. He just walks. Might as well be a horse or a cow or a dog, thinks Garcia, though at least a dog would be company.

Eventually, Wainwright takes a faster pace and walks some distance ahead, consulting his Blacktooth chat device to let base know they're bringing one in. Garcia gives the kid a good look-over; this is his first up close fey encounter since the Incident.

"She wishes to know if you have had success," the creature tells Garcia in a voice so low it's as if it's on a sub-frequency.

Garcia slows his steps. "You *know* me?"

D78 glowers. "I was tasked with seeking you out. Clíodhna wishes to know why you are not helping. Why you hurt us instead."

Garcia's gut turns to stone. This is not a conversation he plans on having with anyone, much less a minion sent from the banshee queen. But just the thought of her again gets his heart racing. "They thought I was *nuts* when I told them what she said," he growls. "Everyone still thinks I'm a sandwich short of a picnic. Tell her thanks—for nothing."

D78 sighs. "So you have abandoned your promise."

"Yeah, well," says Garcia. "Looks like she picked the wrong hero."

Ten weeks ago, the aperture shimmered out of nowhere—Garcia spotted it while stepping off the main road and taking a whiz in the trees. He took a few steps toward it and spotted a face on the other side. Not someone coming through, just a face. And what a face, what a woman. Sculpted cheekbones, green sparkling eyes, long auburn hair. She took a step back so he could see the unbelievable world behind her: verdant grass, a soft cloudless sky, a massive oak. Things that were ordinary, yet surreal. A perfect world, and at the center a shimmering, glorious queen who begged a boon of him—just like in a fairy tale.

Her name was Clíodhna and she required his assistance. *Our world is dying, and we know not why. Our lands and our powers recede daily—leaving only your world behind. Some of our folk have panicked and departed; others are vowing to start a true war with humans if the assaults on those of us who flee continue. Speak to your leaders. Tell them to speak with me. Most of us do not want a battle; that course does not turn out well.*

Then she blew him a kiss, and the scent of fresh-baked bread was replaced with a subtle aroma of roses that wrapped around him like a silken cocoon. "I'll try," he whispered, so in love with her that his insides were on fire. "For you, I'll try."

It should have been easy: he assumed everyone wanted an end to the war, the constant patrolling of the border and processing of creatures. Wouldn't everyone want to know how to stop the fey streaming across the borders, the ones who were making magic and upsetting the locals? They could work together to stop that other world from vanishing. It seemed simple.

It was not.

Garcia thinks about the shimmering airhole he spotted earlier this morning. How it called to him in the seconds before he turned in time to see D78 arriving into his world. He thinks about the kind of guts it takes to dive headlong into a strange land unarmed, and face a world of scared hostiles.

I could have said nothing, thinks Garcia. Instead, he'd done his duty and called out to Wainwright. *I could have let him go.*

"I still want to help," he tells the kid as they walk through the winter-scarred fields. Moist green plants shoot beneath the creature's footsteps, leaving a fragrant trail of spring in his wake. "But I got no idea where to start anymore."

"You may begin by not firing on us," says D78. "That would be most appreciated."

"I have orders," says Garcia, miserably.

"They are not helping," says the creature, and does not speak again.

They put D78 in the truck with all the others rounded up that morning and Garcia watches as it drives off, kicking up dust from the grooves worn in the ground. The covered vehicle bounces back and forth between just two destinations all day, every day: base camp and the holding facility. After that, Garcia has no idea what happens to the creatures.

"Chow?" Wainwright thumbs at the kitchen tent.

"In a couple," says Garcia. "Gonna clear my head."

The lieutenant gives him a narrow-eyed look. "You were having quite a chat with it on the way in here."

Garcia shrugs. Before the Incident being in the field was different: they ran in units of twelve or fifteen, fanning out every morning to mark the grids as cleared and made maps where holes in the air appeared. It was more about surveillance. If they ran into a fey they turned it right around and marched it back to the hole. But D78 hadn't given them any trouble, and they hadn't even tried to find it a hole to go back through.

Back home in Tennessee, Garcia grew up with a rifle in his hands, hunting in the woods for the family supper with his redbone coonhound. Once grown he never thought about doing anything other than soldiering—it's what the men in the family did. But the Peacekeepers didn't feel like soldiering. Their enemy didn't shoot back, rarely even put up a fight. Mostly the creatures were running away from something, and happened to run into you. Now apparently the response was to cart them off to a holding facility and regular EMP pulses until ... until...

Until what? Garcia wonders.

He catches a glimpse of Wainwright going not into the mess, but rather the officers' organizational tent. His hands make fists and his mouth twists.

Where do they send them?

"Douglas," he calls out to a private passing by, gesturing at the truck in the distance. "They got a hole over there to stuff them back in or what?"

"They certainly do," says the soldier.

That surprises Garcia. "Really? A stable portal?"

"Naw," says Douglas. "Ain't no such thing. That way's the pits."

A cool bubble encases Garcia. There's a ring of history to this moment, something from long before even his granddaddy's time. The pits, as far as he's aware, are where you put the bodies—the fey who don't behave. The ones that lob off spells that drive men mad, or turn them into animals, or make them dance until their feet break. Those ones are trouble, and the plasma deals with them fast. You have to put the bodies somewhere, so—pits. But those ones in the truck are like D78. They aren't troublemakers. They're not even dead.

"Sergeant Garcia." Wainwright is calling him, beckoning toward the officer's tent. "You're wanted."

He pulls away from his last thought and summons up the soldier in him. Wainwright, that prick, up to no good.

Inside the officer's tent Colonel Wu is busily signing digital papers that slide across her smartdesk one by one. After a moment she takes a sip of coffee and squints up at Wainwright and Garcia. She nods, and Garcia drops the salute.

"Dismissed, Wainwright."

The lieutenant scurries off, but Garcia imagines him standing just outside the tent flap, listening in.

"Hear you had a conversation with the capture today," says Wu, leaning back and clasping her hands over her chest. She speaks in Mandarin but the Goo-Lexa device next to him spits out the translation almost immediately.

"Yes, ma'am," Garcia nods. It's best not to get into the whys; that's what desked him in the first place.

"You've been out of the field for a while, officer," says Wu. "Seems to me you forgot a few points of order."

Garcia waits, swallowing a number of retorts. "Ma'am?"

"We're reassigning you."

His heart plummets. "Don't take me out of the field, ma'am," he blurts. "I know how to find the airholes."

Wu holds up a hand. "No longer the priority. Too many of them, too many visitors. Now it's triage." She taps on her smartdesk and swipes up Garcia's file. "Right. I thought as much. Time you got a little better education, sergeant. We're done making nice. Unless you want these things striding through your hometown in a couple of months."

Garcia's fingernails dig into the soft meat of his palms. "Ma'am."

"Wainwright will show you where you'll go next. Make the best of it, Sergeant Garcia. We're watching you."

The acrid, burning scent in the air hits Garcia a full klick away, and his eyes are watering by the time the truck comes to a complete stop. Once he disembarks, he can even make out a subtle, curiously pleasant odor of dark chocolate and equally dark beer.

Now that he's at the pitside camp he's outfitted with a shoulder pack, which he slips over his head the way he once did the XL-PEP and goes where he's led mutely. There's a twitch in his gut he's trying not to focus on.

His guide shows him the cages first, portable metal-bar structures pounded into the earth. There are five cells and each is pretty full of fey standing shoulder-to-shoulder. They follow him with their eyes, and he feels the weight of their collective stare as if they are physically on top of him.

Garcia wonders where he went wrong. Then he wonders where *people* went wrong. One at a time, two at a time in the field is one thing. Caging them like animals is—beyond imagining. What are they collecting them for?

A low hum rises in his ears as he nears one particular cage, pulling on him like a divining rod. A hand reaches out and clamps on his wrist.

His guide pulls out a Taser and zaps the owner of the arm, but the grip doesn't lessen. Garcia realizes who it is: D78. "Wait, it's OK," he tells his guide. "Brought this one in earlier."

The guide puts away the Taser. "No touching," he barks at the caged fey, and the fingers release.

D78 stares at Garcia. *Help us*, he hears instead of the hum.

"Get real," he growls under his breath, but there's no heat in it. He can't get over how crowded they are. "Get yourselves out, you're so magic."

More staring. *They fire upon us every hour*, says D78. *There is one we protect from the blasts who can release the lock—but we are weak. And once free we have nowhere to go. Not without assistance.*

"Hey, man, I got things to do," interrupts the guard. "What gives?" A second fey, with bright eyes and a furred face steps forward, brushing its fingers against its lips. The guide's eyes glaze, and he wanders away.

Help us, comes D78's voice. *You are able to find the worn-up places.*

"The airholes?" Garcia swallows. He's oddly tempted by the notion that he could send every one of them back at once—it might put him in the queen's good graces. But he would risk everything by doing it. Anyway, it can't be done. "You'll just come back. And they'll catch you again."

Try, Anthony Garcia. For her. For your promise.

He swallows. "Why can't you just come over here and make nice? Don't do magic?"

Imagine the world if you close your eyes. That is a fraction of what it is like for us when we—blend in. Your kind would ask us to walk in this world blinded and slowly suffocating. And for what?

"I'm not the hero she wants," he says. "I can't fix the world. She wants to make changes, she has to send some help."

D78 looks at him for a beat, long lashes flickering. "What makes you believe she hasn't?" he says out loud, as though to make sure that he's been heard.

Mists rise high and thick the next morning, but they march him to the pits anyway, these vast dugouts in the earth. Steam and heat rise from the interiors like thermal pools, only there's no water at the bottom—just bodies. Garcia raids his satchel and fits on the noseplugs; the stench of death and delightful food odors is a sensory dissonance he can't ignore. He's got a set of noise-blocking earbuds, too, but holds off a moment, listening.

Standing near the lip of one pit, he tunes into atonal, unearthly melodies that float from its interior, sounds both eerily beautiful and like nails dragged across his heart. His stomach roils. A soldier gestures to the far side, where a cageful of the fey stagger up to the lip of the pit.

"The ... music," says Garcia, feeling a tickle in his ears. "What is that?"

The soldier, empty-eyed like most of the others Garcia has seen since arriving, gestures at the pit. "Them," he says. "Not all of 'em die right away. But they can't heal and they can't lob spells at us, so—they sing."

Garcia peers into the pit, squinting—the stacked bodies of the creatures bend and twist over one another, arms akimbo, legs sticking up. None of them rise, but there is a persistent ... movement among them. A squirming. He swipes at his right ear, comes away with a trickle of blood.

"They sing at us until there's nothing left," the soldier goes on in a flat voice. "Once the song stops, we start filling the holes in."

"Why wait?" asks Garcia, faintly sarcastic.

"Wouldn't," says the soldier. "But we can't keep up." He tilts his head. The mists have now cleared and Garcia can take in what he missed before: row upon row of dirt circles, most still open to the air, stretching into the distance.

Garcia's legs buckle and he collapses.

They let him rest in his barracks through lunch, but afterward it's back to the pits—even though he hasn't rested at all. Still dazed and desperate not to be where he is right now, Garcia sticks on the plugs and pops in the earbuds, which filter gentle classical tunes to blot out the discordant music of the dying. It has a calming effect until he realizes it's like being in the world's worst holo-video, with this as his soundtrack.

"Over here," he's told so he listens to the music and goes over there. Other soldiers lead out a fresh queue of prisoners, who make no sound and offer no resistance; Garcia assumes if he'd been hit with that PEP every hour all night he'd be something of a zombie, too.

Remember your promise, comes the voice from the night before and Garcia snaps alive again. He frantically scans the fey, which are now lined up three deep in front of him on the edge of the pit. *We trust you.*

A plasma weapon is thrust into Garcia's hands, and the order counts down to fire. He fails to discharge; can't even bring his finger near the trigger. An officer strides over and smacks him on the back of the head. "Fire, you piece of shit!" he screams. "Think you're better than the rest of us?"

Garcia never looks to see who spoke. When the next order comes he depresses the trigger and holds it down, spraying everything in front of him with the searing plasma. But he does it blindly: he can see nothing, his eyes blurred and streaming.

Remember. Remember.

The bodies fall, and Garcia stops firing only when the voice no longer calls to him.

Left alone in his barracks while everyone else heads off to dinner, Garcia throws the earbuds and noseclip aside and stands next to his cot, shaking. His clothes are filthy, stained with mud splashes and cooked viscera that splattered back when he helped cut the fey bodies down. He tears off the shirt and kicks it under the bed.

Think you're better than the rest of us?

He takes a long, deep breath and realizes he'll never drink beer or eat chocolate again. Or listen to music. That's all ruined. But that's the least important thing. He can't do this day again. He won't.

Better than the rest of us?

"Maybe I am," he says to the empty quarters.

Garcia slips out of the tent and heads directly for the cages full of silent fey. There are two guards, and shift change is imminent; everyone else in camp is at chow.

"Hey," he tells one guard. "I'm up tonight."

"You're not Mendez."

"It's Garcia, you knucklehead," he says. "Our names aren't all the same."

The guard gives him a strange look, but shrugs. "Whatever. Your funeral if you're wrong. I'm starvin' anyway."

Then there is just the one other guard, and he's easily dispatched with a butt to the head that'll leave him with a giant headache in the morning. Not that Garcia plans to be around to find out. Then he goes back to the cages.

"OK," he says. "Do it."

They stare at him mutely.

"Look, I know one of you can open this thing. So do it. We're going."

Every fey turns inward and there is a strange, crackling energy among them. They are speaking, he understands that— but not to him. They turn back and continue to stare blankly.

Shit, thinks Garcia. "Your queen—asked for help. She sent— somebody to help me. He's gone now. We—I—killed him. But … no more. No more." His voice cracks on the last word. He's plead- ing, now. If he has to do this one more day, he'll throw himself in the pit with the others.

We know you, comes a voice. Not D78. Another. *You are not our hero.*

"No," he says. "But I'm all you got."

A long moment of emptiness. Dusk is approaching; night will give them the cover they need to escape. He hopes. They're out here on a countryside plain and no one should notice for an hour, maybe two. That might be enough.

It'll have to be.

Then there's a zap on the keypads of all the cages and the locks open as one. The fey emerge in a shuffling, loose clutch. He backs away until everyone has exited the cages. "I'm sorry," he says.

Take us home, Anthony Garcia.

All at once, that is his only wish.

He slips them around the far side of the cages, then traverses the camp edge with the group as the sky loses its light. The camp is open to the elements, wall-less and gate-less, but he goes cautiously until he is reasonably certain everyone has crossed the perimeter.

Once they are clear, he turns north with a soldier's jog. They race silently behind him, like children following a Pied Piper. But there is no cave to take them to, no safe haven or worn-up place, only the deep, cold water of the Channel some miles ahead— which is farther than Garcia expects any of them will be able to get. He has no plan, only the repeating obsessive knowledge that they need to be *not here*.

So he runs and they run with him into the gathering dark, leaving lush, blooming trails in their wake, a verdant trail of impermanent magic that anyone with eyesight will be able to track. *They are their own worst enemies here*, thinks Garcia. *They don't know how to be anything other than themselves.*

Yet they run with him, tireless, for hours. Eventually when Garcia stumbles, throat parched and chest exploding they scoop him up and carry him into the starry night, continuing their escape to nowhere. Hoping all along that somewhere ahead is a worn-up place in the universe waiting to gather them in its arms and bring them home.

You can't right the wrongs of the whole world," she said.
"All you can do is your very best to make a difference to the
people in front of you right here, right now. Help one person,
and then another, and another. Don't even count them.
Jacey Bedford

The Horse Head Violin

JACEY BEDFORD

I DIDN'T NOTICE HIM UNTIL THE CROWDS OF BELGIAN REFUGEES FROM the train at Queen Street Station had thinned. He was hanging back, his left arm in a sling, thick bandages around his hand. His right hand clutched the hand of a girl of maybe nine or ten years old. "*Voulez-vous une tasse de thé?*" I asked. "*Et ta soeur?*"

"Ja. A cup of tea, thank you."

His voice squeaked, giving his age away. He was probably no more than fourteen.

"You speak English."

"A little." He squeezed the girl's hand. "Tea, Eveline. Say thank you to the lady."

The child looked up at me with eyes round as saucers but said nothing.

"Eveline means to say thank you, miss, but... she's shy." His English was perfectly understandable despite a pronounced accent. He said something in Flemish to Eveline, who released his hand, but clutched the fabric of his coat. I saw that tucked inside his sling was the neck of a violin. The head, usually a scroll, was carved into the face of a woman. There wasn't room for a whole violin inside the sling. It had to be a broken-off neck. I hoped that if he was a musician, his damaged hand would heal so he could play again.

"Do you need to see a nurse?" I pointed to his bandaged hand. "Or a violin maker?"

He shook his head. "The dressing should be changed in three days. Alas the violin..." He shook his head, his slate-grey eyes wet with unshed tears.

His hair was thick and wavy and might be fair when it was clean. His lips were well-shaped, but trembled when he spoke. His sister, Eveline, had the same fair hair. Even taming it into two thick plaits couldn't disguise the natural curl. Her heart-shaped face was solemn, her eyes never still. She glanced about as if looking for something, or someone.

I was seeing first hand the tragedy that I'd read about in the newspaper. Life was never dull in my job as secretary to Mrs. Ratcliffe. She was a society lady, wife of Mr. Charles Ratcliffe, and niece to Mr. Edward Brotherton—former member of parliament and owner of the Brotherton chemical company. He had the honour, if honour it was, to be Lord Mayor of Leeds when the Archduke Franz Ferdinand was assassinated in Sarajevo, triggering a chain of events that led to war. Being a widower, Mr. Brotherton had asked Mrs. Ratcliffe to be his lady mayoress, and she had stepped into the role as if born to it. It was that role that took us to the station. Mrs. R. was always one to lead by example.

Britain entered the war in 1914 when Germany invaded neutral Belgium. Our brave boys, my own brother amongst them, volunteered to fight, thinking it would all be over by Christmas.

Hardly had Tommy kissed me goodbye and set off for Pontefract to join the King's Own Yorkshire Light Infantry, when Mrs. Ratcliffe called me into her study.

"Polly, we are going to welcome the Belgian refugees," she announced. "Your French is passable." Mrs. Ratcliffe, though only about six years older than me, was already a force of nature. She could silence a roomful of chatterers merely by walking into it. If Mrs. Ratcliffe said we were going to welcome refugees, then we were, and so, no doubt, was every lady of quality in Leeds who wanted to earn Mrs. Ratcliffe's approval.

"The Belgian refugees," she continued, "will be arriving by train from Folkestone where they have been obliged to sleep on the beach." I had read the newspaper. On the fourteenth of October, after the fall of Antwerp, sixteen thousand Belgian refugees landed at Folkestone in a single day, and more arrived daily at Tilbury, Margate, Harwich, Dover and Hull. Never had Britain seen such an influx, but Brave Belgium, as a country, was a war hero, standing as it did between the Kaiser's troops and the French border.

Everyone rallied round, donating spare clothes and blankets. The Belgians were being sent inland by the train-load, ill-equipped and traumatised, to be housed in church halls or by families with goodwill and a spare bed.

As the train huffed into Queen Street Station, Mrs. Ratcliffe gave the ladies of the Refugee Committee one last cool stare. "You all know your places and your jobs. Let's do our very best to give these poor souls a warm welcome."

Some of the volunteers had been running around all after-noon trying to reunite husbands with wives, children with parents. We heard an occasional joyous shout when they succeeded.

"Have you lost someone?" I asked the boy as he gave me back his empty cup.

"Ja." He didn't elaborate.

"Maybe the next train?"

He shook his head and squeezed Eveline to him.

"Are you hungry? There are sandwiches."

I saw him begin to frame a polite no thank you, but he looked down at Eveline and nodded.

Ida Lupton, scurried past. "Ooh, my feet are killing me. Mrs. Ratcliffe says there's another train due in ten minutes. I'm not sure how she knows."

"If that's what she says, then there is. The train wouldn't dare be late."

"Mrs. Kitson-Clark says she's a witch," Ida giggled. "How else could she know what she knows and do what she does?"

I put two rounds of sandwiches into a paper bag and handed them over to the young man together with two more cups of tea. "Have they told you where you're staying tonight?"

"Eveline is supposed to go to the Society of Friends and I am to go to the Town Hall."

"They're splitting you up?"

Eveline gave a little mewling cry and clung to her brother's arm, her eyes wild.

He nodded.

"That can't be right," I said. "There are a dozen people whose sole job it to reunite families."

He shrugged. "We will not go." He looked around the station as if looking for a corner to hide in. "We have lost too much. We will not lose each other."

With the toot of a whistle and the screech of metal the next train huffed into the station in a cloud of sulphurous smog.

"Aren't you supposed to be on the platform?" Ida said, retying her apron over her dress.

"I suppose so, though I think I've forgotten most of my French and I don't speak Flemish."

"Do what you did before. Smile and point."

"Polly!" Mrs. Ratcliffe barely had to raise her voice to make herself heard.

I scurried to catch up with her as she sallied forth into the crowd of folks descending from the second train.

I flinched from their dead-eye stares and hesitated.

A firm hand in the middle of my back propelled me forward. "You won't do any good like that, girl," Mrs. R. said.

"I'm not sure how much good I'm doing anyway," I said. "There's so much hurt."

She looked me in the eyes and dropped her voice to a throaty whisper. "You can't right the wrongs of the whole world," she said. "All you can do is your very best to make a difference to the people in front of you right here, right now. Help one person, and then another, and another. Don't even count them. It's not a competition. Small steps, Polly, and you'll walk a long road."

She was right. By the time the second train-load of refugees had been fed, clothed, tended and directed to their next destination, my feet were sore and my back ached, but I didn't feel useless, even handing out cups of tea and smiles. The smiles were most important; even without language they said, *you are welcome. We will take care of you. We can't make up for your loss, but we can help you to go forward from here.*

In the late evening Mrs. R. clapped her hands for our attention. "That's it for today," she announced. "Well done, ladies. There's another train arriving tomorrow at three. Please be here by two-thirty at the latest."

I glanced around to make sure I hadn't left anything behind. It was then I saw a girl peering through a crack in the waiting room door. As our glances connected, a hand appeared around her shoulder and drew her inside. The door closed.

It took me a few moments to place her heart-shaped face. I walked to the waiting room and pushed open the door. There were two figures sitting together on a bench, their backs to me.

"Eveline?"

The child jumped up, startled at the sound of her name. Her brother stood and pushed her behind him. "You can't separate us. We will not go."

I raised both hands, palm outwards. "I'm not here to send you anywhere. Besides, everyone's gone. Why are you still here? Can I help you to find where you should be going? Didn't you say something about the Town Hall? It's not far I can give you directions."

"It's for boys only."

Ah, so that was why they were trying to split up brother and sister.

"So what do you intend to do?"

His grey eyes clouded over and he shook his head. "Maybe tomorrow they will find somewhere where we can be together."

"Where are your parents?"

He shook his head. "We have no one. No one and nothing. Except each other."

"I don't even know your name," I said.

"Verlinden," he said. "Piet Verlinden."

"Pleased to meet you. I'm Polly Daniels."

An idea had been taking shape. I'd have to let someone know tomorrow and see if a permanent place could be found, but for tonight...

"You can come home with me," I said. "My brother Tommy joined up, so you can sleep in his room if you like."

"Say thank you to Miss Daniels, Eveline," Piet said, but Eveline said not one word. "She doesn't mean to be rude, miss. I thank you on her behalf."

We walked home from the station in the deepening dusk, past riverside warehouses and garment factories, and finally up Beeston Hill to Shaw Street, a cobbled cul-de-sac with a long line of back-to-back, brick-built houses. The toilets, earth closets clustered together in a yard, a little further down the street, one for every two houses.

I didn't know how to talk to my charges. Whatever I said was bound to remind them of what they'd been through. I'd lost both my parents, but not in such traumatic circumstances and at least I still had a roof over my head.

It took a while to light the fire and coax it to give out enough heat to boil potatoes on the trivet and to fry sausages on the plate above the side-oven.

As I put the sausages and mash on the table I said, "My brother has joined the army, the King's own Yorkshire Light Infantry. He's already shipped out to France."

"I hope he returns safely," Piet said.

I felt a shiver run down my spine. Mortars and shells had destroyed Piet's home. Tommy would face all that and more.

"They say it will be over by Christmas," I said.

He didn't reply.

"Would you like to put that somewhere safe?" I nodded to the violin head still poking out of his sling.

He drew the intricately carved head out of its hiding place. It still had about six inches of the neck attached but the fingerboard was missing and it had lost all its pegs. Eveline stared at it and whimpered a little when he placed it carefully on the sideboard.

"Do you play?" I asked.

"A little, but my sisters both play better than me."

"Sisters?" The question was out before I'd thought about it.

"Eveline and Marika."

At the sound of her sister's name Eveline whimpered again.

I didn't know what to say, so I said nothing. Eventually the silence worked. "We were told that Zeebrugge was about to fall to the German advance, so we tried to reach Oostende, but then we were directed to Blankenberge. We lost Marika... at Blankenberge..."

Eveline whimpered again.

I gave Piet a pair of Tommy's old pyjamas and Eveline a spare nightdress that buried her.

"I hope you'll be comfortable." I showed them the bedroom, shadowed in the glow from the gas mantle, and pointed out the chamber pot under the bed before retiring to my own room.

I slept fitfully, woken once by Eveline's screams and another time by her brother's low voice and her pitiful sobs.

In the morning the siblings were up before me. By the time I came downstairs, Piet and Eveline between them had persuaded the fire into life and the kettle was already singing on the trivet.

I popped out to visit the necessary and then ran up to the corner shop to buy bread, onions and carrots, and a pound of shin beef from the butcher which would need to simmer all day to make the best of it.

"I have to go to the station again today," I told Piet and Eveline. "But you two can stay here and I will enquire as to whether there's somewhere you can both go together."

"Thank you," Piet said. "What can we do to help?"

"I'm going to make a stew," I said. "You can keep the fire going and make sure it doesn't burn."

"We can do better than that." He waved Eveline to the table. "We will make the stew."

I left them to it and went to join Mrs. R. and the ladies at the station.

When there was a break in the influx of refugees, I told Mrs. R. how I'd acquired my guests and asked if it wasn't a shame to split up siblings just because one was a boy and one was a girl, especially when they'd lost so much already. She took it upon herself to interrogate the accommodations committee, but could find nowhere that my refugees could call home, at least not until Piet's hand healed. When he was fully fit there might be an agricultural job for him which would allow him to take his sister. She did, however, add me to the register of billets, so I could claim a small amount to feed my charges.

Days passed, and it was becoming obvious there was something more than shyness amiss with Eveline.

"Is it that she has no English?" I asked Piet, wondering if she understood what I said.

"She speaks some English," Piet said.

"Pardon me for asking, but did she speak—you know—before?"

"Uncle Henri—he took us in after our parents died—said she never shut up. She and Marika..." He pressed his lips together. "They were twins. It's hard to lose a twin."

"It's hard to lose a sister," I said.

His eyes teared up. I wanted to hug him, but at the age of fourteen he was desperately trying to be the man of the family.

Days passed. Eveline still made no effort to speak, and whenever I asked her a direct question would only nod or shake her head.

One morning I woke early. I thought I was the only early riser, but when I arrived downstairs I saw Eveline, still in her nightdress, sitting on the floor crooning softly over something cradled in her arms. She heard me and started visibly. Tears ran down both cheeks and I swear she looked guilty. She leaped to her feet. I heard something clatter as she ran past me. As her footsteps retreated up the stairs I realised that the object of her sadness and guilt was the carved violin head.

After breakfast, while Eveline visited the necessary, I asked Piet what was upsetting her.

"She misses Marika," was all he would say. By the look on his face she was not the only one.

"Your parents?"

"Died when we were young, and our uncle was killed in the shelling," he said. "He was a good man, and kind to us in his way, though never like a father, if you know what I mean."

Days passed. My refugees settled into a routine, helping with housework and cooking while I was at work.

When the influx of Belgians slowed to a trickle I stopped going to the station and resumed my job with Mrs. R. She and Mr. Brotherton had a new project—equipping the Leeds Pals regiment to go to the front. Perhaps if Tommy had not been so eager to join up, he could have joined the Pals instead of the KOYLI, but it was too late now. I'd had one letter from him so far, complaining about the food and Sergeant Atkinson, but saying he'd made some good mates and they were looking out for each other. They were behind the lines, waiting to be called to the front. I checked the date on the letter. It had been written nearly four weeks ago, so he could be anywhere by now.

Piet made several visits to the first aid station set up for the refugees, but simply shook his head when I asked him how his hand was doing. One week later they sent him up to the hospital and he returned with a grim expression. He'd been told to go the following morning prepared to stay in overnight so they could amputate two of his fingers before he lost his whole hand to infection. I looked at the sad remains of the violin, still on the sideboard. He'd never play again.

Maybe it was time to see if I could acquire an instrument and see if Eveline would play. The broken violin was a focus for her grief. Until she came to terms with whatever was preventing her from speaking she would never begin to heal.

Eveline made no fuss about staying with me while Piet went to the hospital, but in the middle of the night her screams woke me. I called out to her and then finally lit a candle and opened the door to her room. She flung herself into my arms, almost knocking the candle holder from my hand.

"Come on, then." I took her to my room and drew her into bed with me.

Throughout the night she fretted and turned, speaking in sleep as she never did during the day, though I didn't grasp a word of her Flemish.

Piet returned the following afternoon, pale-faced and with even more bandages around his hand.

"They've said it should heal much more cleanly now they've removed two fingers." He stared at the dressing. "I hope they've cut off the right fingers. I can still feel them. I swear they hurt more than they did before. How can they hurt when they're not even there?" He looked at the violin head and shrugged. "We should get rid of that," he said, and picked it up as if about to cast it into the fire.

Eveline flung herself at him screaming. There were no words but her intention was obvious.

The following Monday morning I caught the omnibus to Roundhay Hall. With Piet's permission I took the violin head to show Mrs. R. She had friends who were artists, writers and musicians. I wondered whether she might be able to conjure up a violin, maybe one the Verlindens could borrow.

"That's a lovely carving." Mrs. B. held the broken piece to the light of the window and turned it all round, scrutinising it carefully. "It's unusual. What a shame the rest of the instrument isn't attached. It must have been very fine. What happened to it?"

"I don't know. It means something to both of them, but especially to Eveline. Piet has had two finger amputated, so he'll probably never play the violin again."

"I used to know a piano player who lost his index finger. He learned to play again. He said it's simply a question of retraining the fingers you have left. See how your boy is when he's had the dressings removed. In the meantime let me think about finding another instrument."

Two weeks later I saw Piet's damaged hand for the first time. It made me a bit queasy to look at it, at first, but eventually I stopped noticing the fading scar and the missing fingers. He flexed his remaining fingers one morning, a week after his bandages had been removed.

"It's time to get a job," he said. "We have taken advantage of your hospitality for too long already I believe you said there was a job on a farm where we might both go. I think my hand is good enough to hold a hoe or drive a plough horse."

I'd grown accustomed to having the Verlindens around. I didn't want them to go, but I knew if it was me in their position I would want to make my own way in the world and not rely on charity.

Mrs. R. arranged it. Organising was what she did best. She knew of a farmer out Rawdon way, who would give Piet and Eveline a place and a small wage. The day before they were due to leave, she gave me a violin case.

"For your Belgian friends," she said. "A gift. In exchange for their story."

"It may take a while to get that," I said. "Eveline can't speak about whatever happened, and Piet doesn't want to."

"I'll wait until they are ready," she said. "It's been such a short time. It may take months, or even years."

I opened the case on the omnibus on the way home. It was a beautiful, instrument with the patina of age, and instead of a scroll there was a carved horse's head. Only Mrs. R. could come up with something so beautiful and so unusual in such a short time. I gave it to Piet, explaining that Mrs. R. would very much like to know what had happened to their own violin, but if he didn't want to tell her, that was all right, too.

He opened up the case and simply stared at the lustrous instrument, complete with bow. He stroked it with the fingers of his good hand.

"You might be able to play it again." I told him about Mrs. R's pianist friend with the missing index finger.

"I was never as good as Eveline, and Eveline was never as good as Marika," he said. "They always competed against each other for use of the violin. It was a special one. It had been in the family since our grandfather made it for our grandmother to play. We only had the one instrument, you see, so they could never play duets."

"Did the violin get crushed in the bombing?"

"No," he said. That was it. No further details, but he ran his thumb across the finger-stumps of his left hand, and I could see he was close to tears. Then he kissed the damaged violin head and laid it in the case alongside the new instrument.

"There," he said. "They will make friends and soon the new violin will learn from the old."

Mrs. R. had given me permission to go with Piet and Eveline to their new home the following morning, and she had even sent her own car for us, a Renault, driven by the immaculate, but taciturn Mr. Kay, who was almost as silent as Eveline. It felt very grand to ride in a chauffeur-driven car, but though Kay managed to convey that all three of us were beneath him, he conducted us there in safety and waited while I spoke to the farmer's wife.

Mrs. Goody was a welcoming soul and saw Piet and Eveline to two tiny attic rooms, their new home. Piet would work on the farm and Eveline could attend the village school until she was old enough to work in the dairy. Mrs. Goody's son had joined the Leeds Pals, and her daughter had recently married a young farmer and moved to the next village, leaving the rooms empty.

"It'll be right grand to have youngsters about the place again," she confided in me. "I'll look after 'em, miss, and you can come and visit whenever you like."

As I was about to climb into the Renault, Eveline ran across the yard and flung herself at me. I hugged her, thinking how quickly these two had begun to feel like my own family.

In the weeks that followed I received diligent letters from Piet, always with kisses from Eveline tagged on to the bottom of the page. She still wouldn't speak, but she was getting on well at school, he told me, and there were three other Belgian refugee families in the village.

I visited once a month, on a Sunday, pleased to see that Piet hardly favoured his damaged hand any more, and the fresh air and Mrs. Goody's cooking was starting to put some meat onto his skinny body. Eveline looked the same as ever. Mrs. Goody had taught her to milk already, on the principle that cows always behaved better for women than for men. I don't know if it was truly the case, but I think it gave Eveline a certain pride.

"What job would you have had if you had still been at home?" I asked Piet.

"My uncle was a builder. I would have gone into the family business."

"How about the violin? Is the new instrument learning from the old?"

He winked at me, a genuine sparkle in his eye. "Of course."

"Has she played it yet?"

"Not yet, but she has looked at it, and I think she wants to. She needs to know Marika has forgiven her."

"For what?"

But he didn't reply.

One Christmas came and went, and another. Life settled down. The Belgians in our city and our countryside became a fact of life and we almost ceased to notice them. I walked out with a young man called Edward for a few months. He had not volunteered for the army because his eyesight was poor, but he talked all the time of how glorious it would be to shoot Germans. I'd had letters from Tommy at the front and knew that he was finding it anything but glorious in the trenches, so Edward and I didn't suit each other. We parted amicably, and I concentrated on working for Mrs. R.

In July 1916, on the first day of the Battle of the Somme, tragedy stuck the Leeds Pals, which had by now become the 15th

Battalion (1st Leeds) The Prince of Wales' Own (West Yorkshire Regiment). That was such a mouthful that locally we still called them the Pals. *"We were two years in the making and ten minutes in the destroying,"* one of the few survivors wrote in the Yorkshire Post. Naturally the mood at Roundhay was sombre. So many young lives gone to waste. I was thankful Tommy had joined the KOYLI instead of the Pals.

I kept in touch with Piet and the silent Eveline, of course, though through the later part of 1917 and 1918 my visits to the farm became less frequent. I had a new task—looking after my brother. Tommy had been wounded at Passchendaele in July 1917, half his calf torn away by shrapnel. For some months he stayed in a hospital in Scotland. Towards Christmas they sent him home, limping badly, and suffering from shell-shock. He didn't want to talk about his experiences and sometimes he was silent for so long that I was reminded of Eveline.

At first he could only hobble about on crutches and he had to shuffle up and down the stairs on his bottom, but gradually he improved. He learned to walk on two sticks, and then one, and by October of 1918, no sticks at all, though his middle toes crossed over themselves and his scarred calf wobbled as if it was empty of muscle. He would limp for the rest of his life, but he was alive and he was home, even though he was not the carefree young man who had set off so enthusiastically in 1914.

I had taken Tommy to visit Piet and Eveline a few times and they had developed a cautious friendship. All three of them had seen things which I had not, and I sometimes felt like an outsider in that little group.

Finally, in November 1918, the war that was supposed to be over by Christmas ended—four years and thousands upon thousands of lives too late. Bells rang and newspaper headlines were full of the Armistice, signed at the eleventh hour of the eleventh day of the eleventh month. The end of the 'war to end all wars' brought a mixture of emotions. Joy and sorrow ran hand in hand—joy that it was over, and sorrow for all those who had died, been injured or suffered bereavement and displacement.

Mrs. Goody wrote and invited me and Tommy to a concert in the village hall, to celebrate the armistice. Eveline was playing the violin.

I told Mrs. R. that her violin would be featured in a concert and she insisted on coming herself, so Tommy and I were privileged to ride to Rawdon in the Renault with Mrs. R., and with Kay at the wheel as usual.

Before the concert started I took Mrs. R. backstage and introduced her to Piet and Eveline. She shook hands with Piet and then took Eveline on one side. I didn't hear what she said except for her opening gambit. "You owe me a story, young lady..."

We returned to our seats and sat through the church choir's rendition of soldiers' songs. I felt Tommy shaking with silent laughter by my side.

"They've cleaned that one up a bit," he whispered.

Then it was Eveline's turn. She looked lovely in a white dress as she walked out on to the stage with her violin.

She came to the front, took a deep breath and opened her mouth to speak. I reached out and gripped Tommy's fingers, squeezing them so hard that he winced. I saw Piet in the wings, his eyes wide in surprise.

"My... my brother and I... would like to thank you all for taking us in and making us welcome." She spoke hesitantly at first and her accent was much more pronounced than Piet's. "We wish to thank Polly for her kindness and friendship, and Mrs. Goody for giving us a home. But I especially want to thank Mrs. Ratcliffe for the gift of music. And I owe her a story.

"When we fled from our home, we walked for miles and miles to the coast. The only way we could reach the big ship was by crowding into the little boats rowing out from the beach. It was cold and dark. The waves tossed us about. There were hundreds of us and not enough boats. My brother Piet held my hand and I should have held my sister's hand, but we had our violin to look after, so Marika and I each held the neck, our fingers touching. It was a shared instrument, you understand, and we both squabbled over it endlessly before... before the Germans came. Our boat was too full. In the darkness and confusion Marika fell into the water between our boat and the next. I let go of the violin."

She blinked very slowly.

"I let go."

She took a deep breath. "Piet leaned over the side and grabbed for my sister. He grasped the violin and pulled it up, but she was no longer holding on. The two boats crunched together, the violin and my brother's hand were trapped, and... and... Marika was gone."

The audience sat in total silence, almost as if they held their collective breath.

"I am going to play a tune for my sister." She looked up. "I'm sorry, Marika. I should have held on tighter."

Then she began to play.

I don't know if the new instrument had learned from the old one, or if it had always sounded so lovely, but when Eveline played it all the sorrows of the world welled behind the music. Some of the gruff country farmers were wiping their eyes. Then the melody transformed from unbearable sadness to joy. In it I heard two carefree sisters arguing over whose turn it was to play and their delight in the music, first from one sister and then from the other. It was as if Eveline poured her grief, held in for so long, on to the stage.

When the last note rang out into the hall, the audience sat transfixed, as if shocked into silence. Then the place erupted into tumultuous applause. Mrs. Ratcliffe stood, and the rest of the audience followed suit.

After the concert, Piet and Eveline came out into the hall. Mrs. Ratcliffe leaned forward and kissed the girl's cheek. "Thank you. Payment gratefully received."

"Did you know she was going to do that?" I asked Piet.

He shook his head. "I only knew she was going to play. I never dreamed. Your Mrs. Ratcliffe is a magician."

"Someone once told me she was a witch." I said. "I'm glad she's on our side. She knows how to get what she wants, and she persuades other people to do her bidding while thinking it was their idea all along."

"It is a great gift."

"What will you do now the war is over?" I asked. "Will you stay or will you go home?"

"Your own young men are coming home from the front. They will need their homes, jobs, space to breathe, time to forget about the horrors they have seen. I recommend a job in the country."

He glanced across at Tommy who was talking to Mrs. Goody. "Your brother could do worse than come and work here when we leave."

"You're already planning to go."

"I am good with my hands, even though I don't have quite enough fingers. My father and my uncles were builders. We will go home and rebuild."

Piet and Eveline stayed with Mrs. Goody for one last Christmas, and in early January 1919 Tommy and I went with them to Leeds Station to wave goodbye as they set out for home.

I remembered the day I'd first seen them, such a long time ago.

"Write to me," I told Piet.

"Of course we will," he said. "You'll never be far from our thoughts."

Eveline hugged me. "Thank you, Polly," she whispered in my ear. "You are my big sister now."

And with that they were on the train, disappearing in a cloud of steam and coal dust, Tears ran down my face. I was too stunned to even wipe them away. Her big sister!

Two hundred and fifty thousand Belgian refugees came to Britain during the war, and within a year of the armistice, ninety percent of them returned home to rebuild. They vanished as if they had never been...leaving behind only a memory of a melody played on a horse head violin.

"Damn all of you who think that killing a flower will kill the memories of a nation. We will survive. We will endure. We leave our bones and our graveyards and our dead behind us, because we must. But we carry the memories within us."
Alma Alexander

The Bones of Our Ancestors, the Blood of Our Flowers

ALMA ALEXANDER

THEY PASSED LIKE SHADOWS IN THE NIGHT, THE TWO OF THEM—THE old man with a mattock slung over his shoulder and the boy with an empty sack dangling from one hand. The old man's eyes sometimes caught what little moonlight there spilled from the waning moon in the clear sky above as he glanced around him watching for other moving shadows; the hand resting on the handle of his mattock seemed casual but in fact everything about him was tense, wary, waiting for unseen danger. The boy swung from trudging along dutifully and stifling a yawn every so often to occasionally catching his companion's mood and looking around in the abrupt panic-stricken manner of a startled rabbit.

Nothing else moved in the night except the two of them, but the old man clung to the edge of the trees and what concealment they offered, and did not break out into the open field until he absolutely had to. Even then, he hesitated for the longest time, raking the trees and the meadow for danger before he stepped out into the open.

"Come," he whispered, speaking for the first time. "Hurry. We have little time."

The boy yawned. "Grandfather, why are we..."

"Hush. If you do not understand already, now is not the time. Stay alert."

"What are we looking for?"

The old man paused for a moment, glancing up at the sky. "Once, perhaps, angels," he said abruptly. "Tonight, who knows what demons walk. Follow. Be quiet, and be wary."

They stepped out into the grass, and a cool breeze they had not felt under the trees reached out to caress their cheeks, wrapped stray blades of the long grass around their ankles.

"How do you know where to look?" the boy said, dropping his voice even lower. "There's a whole field..."

We know. We have always known. This is your blood, your heritage, you should be able to walk on this field and find what we've come here to seek without pause, without thinking. I could have—I could have, if only these old bones did not get in the way... this belongs to both of us, boy. This is our past... but this is your future...

The old man's thoughts were harsh... but he had said nothing. Not out loud. And the silence settled on both of them, gently, like the touch of a moth's wings. And out there on the field, in the dimness of the pallid moonlight and the glitter of distant stars, the grasses shimmered and stirred, as if the field were breathing. No, as if it were holding its breath...

The boy swung the empty sack he carried. "Grandfather," he said carefully, "it's *bulbs...*"

The old man's eyes glinted again as he turned briefly to glance at his grandson, and this time the glint was more than just moonlight on a reflective surface. This time it was moonlight on water. The old man's cheeks were streaked with tears, and more brimmed in the corner of his eye. "Some day," he whispered, turning away again. "Some day, you will understand. These are the bones and the blood of our ancestors..."

The boy suddenly flung out a pointing finger, squinting into the half-light. "What's *that?*"

The old man followed the line of the boy's hand, allowed his gaze to linger on what looked like freshly turned earth, bitter evidence of what other men who had walked abroad this night had already done here. His shoulders sagged, his mattock slipping down along his arm and into the ground at his feet, burying itself lightly into the earth. The old man leaned on it heavily, as though he suddenly could not stand unaided any more.

"They appear to be gone," he whispered brokenly. "But not before they finished their dirty work tonight. Go, you, my boy. Go, and tell me if what I fear is true. Go, go over there, and tell me what you see."

The boy hesitated, spooked by the way in which his grandfather had apparently aged twenty years or more in the space of a single instant, and then crept forward slowly, his hand tight around his sack.

It was hard to make it all out in the wan moonlight, but he could see enough. The earth looked as if it had been chewed by a hungry dragon, hewed and pitted with small holes, the grass mashed under booted feet and giving off an odour of wounded green, small piles of soil scattered around. Something that looked either makeshift-primitive or broken, obviously an implement used to dig all these holes in the ground, lay discarded a little way off; so did something else, something metallic, something that caught the moonglint and even half hidden by grass and soil gleamed with a pale evil glow. The boy stepped over gingerly to take a better look and saw a folding pocket knife, its blade snapped in half, lying next to something else, something he could not, in the first moment, make out.

And then he did, and frowned.

"They chopped it up," he said, his voice louder than he intended, too loud in the quiet darkness. "They hacked it up—they diced it, and then they seem to have... ground it under their heel..."

The old man lifted his face to the sky, raising one hand, his fingers curled into a savage fist. "Damn you," he said softly. "Damn you all, you bastards, you bandits. You may think you came when nobody was looking but God sees. God knows. Your reward is coming, so help me. It is coming. Are they all gone, boy? All dead? All the bulbs?"

The boy suddenly found that he was crying, without quite knowing why, astonished that he could weep at the death of a few dug-up flower bulbs as though they had been children hewn down by a barbarian invasion. He had not really thought about any of this when his grandfather had hoisted him out of bed that night to come on this expedition. He was of a different generation, all his own experiences being fury and loathing which was more often than not based on the name he bore and not on what or who else he might have been. All he could think of, as he was being shaken awake, was that their bags had been packed for days awaiting their departure, and they were *leaving* this place, leaving behind the fear and hatred that had festered between the two warring peoples who claimed it, one by virtue of history and blood-ties and heartland and the other by right of superior numbers—leaving behind its heavy twin legacies of death and of triumph, finally leaving, finally free—but that was not why his Grandfather had woken him. They were not leaving yet. This place was not done with him yet, and the memories came flooding back.

He remembered his grandmother, gone these many years, with scarlet flowers in her hand. He remembered the way she held them, gently, worshipfully, as though they were precious. He remembered his grandfather coming in out of the summer sunshine and seeing the woman and the flowers and making a sign of blessing upon both the flowers that grew on this field, and no other. The flowers dyed scarlet by the blood of warriors six hundred years dead. Somehow, he remembered that too—the fierce sounds and stomach-turning stench of ancient battle where blood flowed under swords and horses screamed as they died and vows were being kept or broken and a nation hurled itself on the point of history and... what... even six centuries later it was still hard to tell whether they had perished utterly or won themselves a place in the eternal memory of the world. Such is the thin line between heroism and lunacy, between legacy of pride and legacy of hubris. The boy was part of his past, as all men are.

And now, finally, standing here over the shattered bulbs, he suddenly realised what they were and why his grandfather had come here this night.

Standing here, in the open field in the dark hours before his last dawn on the ancestral land for which his forebears had fought and bled and died... he remembered it all, somehow. Remembered the sight and the smell and the bright colour of the blood of a battle that had shaped a nation, blood which had seeped into the ground here and, legend had it, dyed the flower called the *bozur*, which his grandmother had worshipped, to the blood-red which they were to this day.

"All of them?" his grandfather said again. "Is there not one...?"

The boy bent down to bring his eyes closer to the ground, peered at the dug-up earth at his feet. What he could see of the destroyed bulbs made him feel oddly queasy; they looked... wounded, like a human being would have looked wounded. Like a child would have. As though limbs and bones had been hacked apart, as though eyes had been gouged out. Worse—as though these were just potential limbs and bones and eyes. As if he was watching the murder of something yet unborn.

"Would they grow from just a piece of it, grandfather?"

"They may, if it was big enough and not too badly damaged," the old man said. "I don't know. I don't know. Oh, cursed... cursed is the land whose very flowers are damned for existing..."

You should know. This is your blood, your heritage. You should be able to walk on this field and find them without pause, without thinking—this is your heritage, boy.

These were words his grandfather had not uttered out loud to him—not here, not on this field, not this night. But somehow he heard them, clear and carrying like the pealing of the bells in the tower of the orthodox cathedral—another thing they would be leaving when the day broke, a thing that the boy had never even thought about before, not consciously, but which he now missed with a fierceness he had not believed possible—and he had not even left it yet. But the words echoed within him, inside a great empty hollow space. They would leaving so much that day—that very morning, in fact, and it would be a race for the boy and his grandfather to be back in their home before it was time to leave it forever. They would be leaving... everything behind. Their home. Whatever they could not carry from that home with them in their luggage, in their hands. The bells ringing out from the domed orthodox monasteries and churches built according to plans brought all the way from Byzantium, with now fading frescoes of ancient saints painted nearly a thousand years before. The bones of his grandmother and his father, in their tombs in the church yard. The dog which had grown up with the boy, and which was already handed over to someone else to take care of, a new home, a new home apart.

Their home. Their dead. Their past.

But not all. Dear God, not all. There had to be one left whole. *One.* His grandfather had said that he should be able to tell...

Blindly, with nothing but instinct and memory and pain, the boy fell onto the violated ground and crawled forward on his hands and knees, heedless of the mess the raw earth was making of his clothes, his fingernails crusted with dirt—feeling, questing, reaching out for that part of himself that was buried in this hallowed ground. One. *One.* One had to have survived this senseless destruction—flower bulbs, hacked and destroyed because they were perceived as having a nationality, a bloodline, a legendary provenance which could not be allowed to exist in the new world of the morning—because the new masters of this place could not allow them to exist. Could not allow it because every scarlet bloom that raised its heavy head denied their own right to this place—because they had no connection with a flower that grew only here, and another people did, the people from whom the land had been taken and stolen and wrested and torn, the people whose blood had continued to feed the red flowers for many years while they were systematically hounded and bullied and murdered off their land.

One. *One.* His grandmother's hands had flowed with them once. One had to remain.

He stumbled over a mound of dirt, and his wrist folded, pitching him forward into as yet untrampled grass. He lay there as though dead for a moment, his fingers twisting painfully around two handfuls of grass, his face on the ground, his mouth open and his lips touching the soil as though he was kissing it. And then a strange feeling coursed through him, as though something electric had reached out and burned him. He pushed himself off the ground with one hand, allowing the other to uncurl, to lie flat beside the clump of grass which it had grasped so violently a moment ago. For a moment he sat there, quite still, and then he began to burrow into the soil carefully, using only his hands. He pushed it aside, right and left, gently, his touch as light as if he was caressing his mother's hand.

And then held his breath as something began to emerge from the dirt. An irregular bulb. Unharmed. Whole.

Holy.

He dug around some more, carefully, freeing it from the hold of the earth, and then he stumbled to his feet, his hands dark with dirt, smears of it on his cheek and the corner of his mouth and clinging to his hair, holding something between his palms as a man might hold water in the desert.

"I found one," he whispered. His voice was very soft, almost no more than a breath, but his grandfather's head turned in his direction. The old man said nothing, but his shoulders tensed and he straightened up, resting only one hand lightly on the mattock.

"I found one," the boy repeated, holding out the bulb.

"Then it is blessing enough," the old man finally said, as though the words were wrung from him. "Bring it. We will make sure the memory lives on."

It was still full night, but away to the east there was the barest hint of a lightening in the sky, the promise of the morning to come. The old man turned to the east and lifted his fist again, a gesture more of a curse than of lamentation now.

"Damn you," he said softly, speaking to the glow in the sky. "Damn all of you who think that killing a flower will kill the memories of a nation. We will survive. We will endure. We leave our bones and our graveyards and our dead behind us, because we must. But we carry the memories within us." He glanced back to where the boy was making his way back with his prize still cradled between his hands like the most precious of jewels. "We will remember," the old man said. "We will remember. As long as that flower blooms. And there will always be one. There will *always* be one."

He allowed his arm to slip briefly around the boy's shoulders as he came near enough, and let his hand convey his pride and his approval, tightening momentarily and then letting go.

"Come," he said. "They will be abroad tonight. And tomorrow, we go. Tomorrow... we go." He swallowed, looking around him at the empty field in the moonlight and shadow, and the boy could see that for the old man it was not empty at all, it was filled with ghosts, with memories, with a long and bitter past. "The best of it... we will take with us," he said softly. "One of them lives."

"I will protect it, grandfather," the boy said, and knew he meant far more than mere words conveyed.

His grandfather understood it, too. Their eyes met, briefly, and then slid apart again.

"Come," the grandfather said, hoisting his mattock back on his shoulder, and deliberately turning back on the violated ground in the field. "Home. Be quiet. Be wary."

They slipped back into the shadows of the trees, and vanished into them.

The breeze stirred the grasses in the Field of Blackbirds, raising a susurrus, a whisper of vanished voices. Ghosts of slain humans and scythed flowers met and mingled in the empty air.

How can you tell me that the only way to live... is to die?
Nora Saroyan

How Can You Tell Me?

NORA SAROYAN

HOW CAN YOU TELL ME HOW CAN YOU TELL ME HOW CAN YOU TELL ME

How can you tell me to adapt? To belong? There is a sound of a different language still whispering in my ears. It is impossible not to listen. It is still the only language I instinctively understand. It is the only language in which I do not begin sentences with, "How you say..."—the only language in which I can still recognize myself.

I understand more than I can say, though. I hear things. I heard two people—not us, two of them, of the here-born, not the ones who drifted in on the storm like us—two of them waiting in line behind us as we stood clutching our shopping cart. They were not loud, but neither were they whispering, and I heard.

"You let them in, and what happens? Have you seen this market lately? Every third woman is not normal any more. All covered up. Like that lot in front."

"And always so many kids with them..."

There were seven of us there that day. My mother, her friend, myself and my baby sister, the other woman's three children, one of them barely older than my babe-in-arms sister, the other two bracketing me in age. It must have been fairly clear we weren't all the children of the same woman. And even if we were...

"Are they talking about us?" my mother said to her friend, very softly, speaking our own language. "I am still not sure— sometimes I miss the middle word and it all turns into nonsenses..."

"They said you aren't normal," I said, in *theirs*.

The two men looked startled, and then their lips thinned in disapproval, and their eyes glittered oddly. With a hard edge to it.

"Quiet," my mother said apprehensively. "Don't make them mad."

"There was that time, last week—when some of them—they—" The other woman had begun to stammer, her words tangling with one another in sudden fear.

"Just stop talking. Just pay, and let us get away safely."

We would have to catch the tube back to the outer levels where our quarters were—the cheap rooms, where gravity was sometimes low or cut out completely without warning for anything from a couple of breathless seconds to long minutes during which you had to scramble to get out of the way of anything that happened to float free in the cutout.

I don't think those men behind us in the queue at the market had ever experienced a gravity cut. Or would know how to deal with it.

It made me feel superior. They would have seen that in my face. They would have resented it. I knew that. I kept my eyes lowered, looking down at my feet. It would not do to make them any madder. There was the tube ride and anything could still happen. Anything at all.

"They don't even make an effort," one of the men said, clearly, loud enough for us to hear as we were leaving, meant for us to hear. "They just come here and expect to carry on exactly as always. There's a reason their world..."

And by then we were out of earshot, thankfully. My mother walked very quickly, and I could see that her shoulders were tense underneath her shawl.

She had been told before, by *them*, that the shawls were an affectation, up here in the station. We weren't on a world surface. There was no wind here. No climate. Nothing to "protect" against. So wearing them—continuing to wear them—*they* took the shawls personally, in some way. As though the women who wore them did so as a gesture of defiance, a thumbing of the nose, a statement that they would never willingly blend in, assimilate, become one of *them*.

But that was what we were meant to do, supposed to do, expected to do. Assimilate. They had given us a refuge and in return we were supposed to shed everything that had once made us who we were, and become thin carbon copies of *them*. We were supposed to think like them, behave like them, look like them, believe like them. There was no room for our shawls on the station, let alone our gods.

Adapt, they said. Belong. Particularly to us, the young ones, the ones whom they could see catching young, making sure of.

Adapt. Change. Belong.

Reject what you brought here. Take up this new thing. Be one of us. Be one of us or stay one of them but if you stay one of them you will never be one of us.

How can you tell me how can you tell me how can you tell me...

I wore the medallion with the face of the Spirit of the Winds, tucked away underneath the clothes they had given me, against my bare skin, against the place where my heart still beat in memory of the grandmother who had given me the medallion—the grandmother who had not made it out with us. She wasn't even buried properly, down there, on the surface of a world pounded into dust. She couldn't have been; there was nobody there to do it. But she sent us away, told us to go, while we still could. She died so we could have a chance at life. Could she have had any idea that the price of survival would mean forgetting her, renouncing her?

Would I be any different if I took her medallion from its place next to my heart and threw it away, and pretended that I had never heard the voice of the Spirit of the Winds howling outside while I was safe and snug and protected in my grandmother's house? Would I be any better? Would I suddenly speak *their* language without an accent to mark me? Would my hair be lighter, and my eyes less hooded, and my face a different color, a different shape? Would that matter?

Would that be easier, to live like that?

Should I buy hair dye in the store and bleach my hair, should I put in contacts that changed the color of my eyes (my grandmother's eyes, they said)—should I cut my hair like the station women did, or wear all those rings like they did in their multiply pierced ears? Should I pay for life by changing,

changing utterly? Would it be surviving if none of the original me actually remained?

"Should I use their words?" I asked my mother at night, repeatedly, as she tucked me into my narrow cot. "Dream their dreams?"

"I don't know, *shallah*, little darling. I don't know. I don't know what is best. Just try and stay out of trouble, don't get into their sights..." She sighed, smoothing my long hair, escaping from its braids like it usually did moments after it was bullied into a semblance of order. "I just want you to remember that..."

"Remember what?" I asked, waiting for the words that never came.

"Just don't forget," she said. "Don't become a stranger."

Some of the other children, the older children, the ones more easily swayed by the opinions of their peers, had done that already. They had become louder, more dismissive, more given to cutting remarks or to simply rejecting things by acting out against them. Many wore the earrings already. It was the price of being even remotely accepted by *them*. And it was easy to understand why. On a world, there would be room to move away or move apart if one needed to, and stay oneself. Here, on the station, there was nowhere else to go. It was life under an inexorable pressure. They couldn't afford to have anybody up here who was different, because different meant dangerous, different meant that someone might not have the bone-deep understanding of station security protocols, someone might leave an airlock open by accident, or crack an air hose, or block a ventilation tunnel, or muck about with the gravity generator.

Everyone had to be the same here, to adapt, to belong.

They hadn't wanted to take us—but there was nowhere for us to go. Not yet anyway. So there we were, occupying the quarters nobody else wanted because gravity was iffy there, grudgingly given the worst jobs on the station which nobody else wanted to do because they were too dirty or too dangerous and paid less for doing them than *they* might have been paid because after all they were already paying us. By giving us a place to alight, by giving us 'sanctuary'. No matter how unwillingly, no matter how easily it might be withdrawn at any time at all, no matter that the price of staying on would mean... giving up identity. Forgetting the way we cooked and ate, the songs we sang, the gods who had walked amongst us.

Forgetting the language we still dreamed with, the language in which some of us would always dream.

Adapt. Belong. Blend in. Release the dangerous differences. Become enough like us to become indistinguishable from us. Only then can you be trusted. Maybe. Perhaps.

Maybe not even then. Not ever. People who were not-us. Not-from-here. People who might never lose their accents, who could never lose the color of their skin, or the texture of their hair, or the haunted look that lurked in the back of their eyes. And how could they be expected to live with that? With the constant reminder of the wars which destroyed worlds, the war which had destroyed our world, the war that could so easily, so easily, come to roost here and wreck the fragile existence they led up here in the station drifting in the stars?

How can you tell me how can you tell me how can you tell me

How can you tell me what to remember, what to forget? How can you tell me how to stop being *me*?

If you ripped the medallion which bears the image of a holy Spirit that once walked our world from its resting place around my thin little neck, would that help you feel less afraid? Would it help if you saw the medallion flung out through that airlock door, and then drifting gently and weightlessly away into infinity, banishing forever the spirits which you have never seen or heard, never known, will never understand?

Unless I do what you tell me, would it help you feel any better if you hadn't taken the medallion away, had simply tossed me away, myself, while I was still wearing it? Whose fear is greater, mine, that I might not be permitted to hold on to anything of my own, or yours, that my being permitted to do so might somehow endanger or even just irrevocably taint everything that is yours?

You are the one with the power here. In the school rooms to which we are sent, the children of the migration with our hidden medallions held tightly and secretly where nobody can see them, we are told how to change, how to become easier for the station which gave us sanctuary to handle, to bear. You don't tell us how to do that without killing the people who we already were, the people who we might have one day become had things been different for us... and become reborn into creatures which you aren't afraid of, creatures which you can take in and assimilate into this machine which gives you all life. Change, and we get to drift closer to the center, where the 'real' people live. Don't change, and we get to drift in microgravity in the outer levels until our bones turn brittle and our eyes turn dim. Adapt, or die. The price of life... is memory, and identity, and all the dreams that once came in a language that *they* do not understand.

How can you tell me...

You can't. You never can.

I will smile. And I will learn to speak without the accent that marks my kind. And I will not take up the shawl that my mother wears, and I might even have my ears pierced.

But my grandmother's medallion... I will take inside me, and carry in my heart, in a place where you can never rip it from me. And the Spirit of the Winds will always be a whisper in the deepest places of my mind, and walk beside me, and be my friend. In time, I will learn how Her voice can help me move the stars themselves.

I know you fear this.

But you should not.

How can you tell me to accept my extinction in order to ensure my continued existence...?

Here, a promise. In return for this place of safety in a world gone to ruin, I will offer a gift in return. In a language you may never understand, I will tell you what it feels like to stand with your feet on the ground, in the dust; I will tell you of what it feels like to lift your face up and feel the rain come spilling down over your closed eyelids, down your cheeks; I will tell you what it feels like to have the Spirit tug at your shawl with her fingers, with the wind of the open country swirling around you; I will tell you what it feels like to dip your hand into a pool that was made by the gods and not by your doing, and drink the water that was the gift that those gods have granted to you. I don't know if you understand that these are treasures, all these sensations, the knowledge of all these things. But they are only treasures if I am permitted to hold on to them, to remember them, to know them, to share them. If you dismiss them and deny them and demand that I abandon them they become worthless to both of us. And if I am to be empty, then the place of safety you offer... comes at too high a price.

How can you tell me that the only way to live... is to die...?

Their people couldn't handle the realization that it was over, that Driftwood was their present and their future, until the last scraps of their world shrank and faded away.
Marie Brennan

Into the Wind

Marie Brennan

THE TENEMENTS PRESENTED A BLANK FACE TO THE BORDER: AN
unbroken expanse of wall, windowless, gapless, resolutely blind
to the place that used to be Oneua. Only at the edges of the
tenements could one pass through, entering the quiet and
sunlit strip of weeds that separated the buildings from the world
their inhabitants had once called home.

Eyo stood in the weeds, an arm's length from the border. The
howling sands formed a wall in front of her, close enough to
touch. They clouded the light of Oneua's suns, until she could
barely make out the nearest structure, the smooth lines of its
walls eroded and broken by the incessant rasp of the sands. And
yet where she stood, with her feet on the soil of Gevsilon, the air
was quiet and still and damp. The line between the two was as
sharp as if it had been sliced with a razor.

"I wouldn't recommend it, kid."

The voice was a stranger's, speaking the local trade pidgin.
Eyo knew he was addressing her, but kept her gaze fixed on the
boundary before her, and the maelstrom of sand beyond. She
didn't care what some stranger thought.

People came here sometimes. Not the Oneui—not usually—
but their neighbors in Gevsilon, or other residents of Driftwood
looking for that rare thing, a quiet place to sit and be alone. The
winds looked like their shrieking should drown out even thought,
but their sound didn't cross the border, any more than the sand
did. As long as you didn't look at them, this place was peaceful.

But apparently the stranger didn't want to be quiet and alone.
In her peripheral vision she saw movement, someone coming to

stand at her side, not too close. Someone as tall as an Oneui adult, and that was unusual in Driftwood.

"You wouldn't be the first of your people to try," he said. "You're one of the Oneui, right? You must have heard the stories."

Oh, she had. It started as a dry, stinging wind, after their world parched to dust. Then it built into a sandstorm, one that raged for days without pause, just as their prophecies had foretold. Eyo's grandparents and the others of their town had refused to believe it was the end of the world; in their desperation, they gathered up their water and food and tied themselves together to prevent anyone from getting lost, and they went in search of a place safe from the sand.

They stumbled into Gevsilon. And that was how they found out their world *had* ended.

But not entirely. This remnant of it survived, caught up in the cluster of fragmented realities known as Driftwood: the place worlds went to die. Gevsilon, their inward neighbor, had gone through an apocalypse of its own: a plague that rendered all their people sterile. There weren't many of the Nigevi left anymore, which meant there was enough room for the Oneui to resettle. Just a stone's throw from the remnants of their own world, and everything they'd left behind.

Of course some of them tried to go back. The first few returned coughing and blind, defeated by the ever-worsening storm. The next few stumbled out bloody, their clothing shredded and their flesh torn raw.

The last few didn't return at all.

"Why do you lot keep trying?" the stranger asked. "You know by now that it won't end well. Is this just how your people have taken to committing suicide?"

Some worlds did that, Eyo knew. Their people couldn't handle the realization that it was over, that Driftwood was their present and their future, until the last scraps of their world shrank and faded away. They killed themselves singly or *en masse*, making a ritual of it, a show of obedience to or protest against the implacable forces that sent them here.

Not her.

She meant to go on ignoring the stranger. It wasn't any of his business why she was here, staring at the lethal swirls of the sandstorm. But when she turned to go, she saw him properly: a tall man, slender and strong, his hair and eyes and fingernails pure black, but his skin tinged lightly with blue.

In Driftwood, people came in all sizes and colors and number of limbs and presence or lack of horns and tails. Eyo didn't claim to know them all. But she'd heard of only one person fitting this man's description.

"You're Last," she said. Sudden excitement made her tense.

His eyes tightened in apprehension, and he retreated a careful step. "I am."

"You can help me," Eyo said.

He retreated again, glancing over his shoulder, toward the faceless wall of the Oneui tenements, and the nearest opening past them. "I don't think so, kid. Sorry. I—"

She stepped forward, matching him. She didn't have her full growth yet, but she was quick and good at running; she would chase him if he fled. "You're a guide, aren't you? Someone who knows things, knows where to find things."

He stopped. "I—yes. I am."

One of the best in Driftwood, or so people said. He knew the patchwork of realities that made up this area, because he'd been around for longer than any of them. The stories claimed he was called Last because he was the last of his own world—a world that had been gone for ages.

Clarity dawned. "Oh. You thought I was going to ask you to go into the sandstorm?"

He gave the howling storm a sideways glance. "You wouldn't be the first."

Because the stories also said he couldn't die. Eyo scowled. "Someone asked you? Who? Tell me their name. I don't care what the storm is like; the idea of sending an *outsider* in there, asking them to bring back the—"

She cut herself off, but not before Last's eyebrows rose. "Bring back? You lost something in the storm?"

"It isn't lost," Eyo snapped. "We know exactly where it is."

Now she saw clarity dawn for *him*. "That's why your people keep going in," he said thoughtfully, gaze drifting sideways again.

"Look, whatever it is—it may not even be there anymore. This is Driftwood; things crumble and fade away, even without apocalyptic sandstorms to scour them into dust."

Conviction stiffened Eyo's crest, her scalp feathers rising in a proud line. "Not this. Everything else will fall apart and die, but not—" She swallowed and shook her head. "When we are gone, this will remain."

His shrug said he didn't agree, but he also didn't care enough to argue anymore. "So if you don't want to send me into that, what *do* you want me for?"

Eyo smoothed her crest with one hand, as flat to her skull as she could make it. If he knew her people, he would recognize that as a gesture of humility and supplication. "I want you to help me find a way to survive the sand."

"I told you it wouldn't work!"

In his fury, Last kicked the wall, which earned him a swift glare from Uaru. Eyo's grandaime had helped build this tenement with their own hands after the Oneua fled the sands. If Last broke something, they would take it out of his hide.

He gestured in apology, and Uaru went back to bandaging Eyo's fingers, their touches as gentle as possible. Eyo bit her lips until she was sure she could speak without hissing in pain. "You said it *probably* wouldn't work. I had to make sure."

"By sticking your hand across the border and letting it get torn apart? Use some common sense, In–Eyo! Get yourself a hunk of meat, wrap *that* up in the slidecloth, and see how it fares before you risk your own flesh!"

She hadn't thought of that. Her hand throbbed under Uaru's ministrations, as if in reproach. By the Oneui's best guess at keeping their old calendar, Eyo was an adult now; she'd gone through her rite of passage two triple cycles of Gevsilon's moons ago, with Uaru and Eyo's other hanaime kin drumming and singing the traditional songs. But Last still called her In–Eyo, as if she were a child, and it was hard to tell him to stop when she'd just done something that proved him right.

"I'll be more careful next time," she said.

Last scowled. "If you had any sense of self-preservation, there wouldn't *be* a next time. In–Eyo—Sa–Uaru—won't one of you tell me what's in there? What are you so desperate to retrieve?"

Uaru pressed their lips together and shook their head. They'd been furious when they found out the person who asked Last to go into the storm was another hanaime, Aune. But even Aune hadn't told Last what they were looking for—not after he refused to go.

Eyo's hand was fully bandaged. She cradled it gently after Uaru released her and began putting away their supplies. "It's something important, Sa–Last. Something we need. Our people never would have left it there if they'd realized . . ."

Her throat closed, ending the sentence. *If they'd realized they could never go back.*

She'd grown up on stories of all the things her grandparents had left behind, everything from shell cameos of ancestors she'd never met to her grandfather's favorite chair. The things they brought with them had the aura of holy relics—even the mundane ones, like the battered tin cup out of which Eyo's grandaime drank their salt tea every morning. But one absence loomed larger than all the rest, not because people spoke of it so often, but because they *didn't.*

Last turned away and braced his palms against the wall, head down. Eyo's hand throbbed again as he watched him. Finally, breathing out a long sigh, he said, "I'll keep looking. Slidecloth obviously isn't enough to protect you. And you would have been walking blind anyway, with that over your eyes. You need something better."

"Thank you," Eyo said.

He straightened up, his air of determination returning. "Thank me by being less reckless with the next possibility."

But the next possibility, when it came, couldn't be tested with a piece of meat.

Last handed over the package with something less than confidence. "You know, normally when a Sut–kef–chid is trying to sell you something, they praise its qualities to the skies. When she heard what I wanted this for, though, she got a *lot* less enthusiastic."

Eyo unwrapped the cloth, revealing a small ceramic flute. "This should calm the winds?"

"It *does* calm winds. And it works outside of Sut–ke; I tested it. But whether it's strong enough to overcome the sandstorm… the only way to find that out is to test it."

Which meant playing the flute. While standing in the storm.

Last's hand twitched. He clearly regretted giving her the flute. Eyo said, "I'm not as foolish as I used to be. Can you get me more slidecloth?"

It wouldn't protect her against the winds for long; she'd proved that three lunar years ago. But it could buy her some time. "I'll see what I can do," Last said.

Wrapped in slidecloth, with a rope harness tied around her body and the flute in her hand, Eyo faced the sandstorm again. Someone had built a bridge over what remained of the Eckuoz Sea at the beginning of the last solar year, widdershins of Oneua and Gevsilon; it turned the weed–filled gap between the window-less backs of the Oneui tenements and the sandstorm into a thoroughfare for people in that part of Driftwood. Garbed and harnessed as she was, Eyo garnered a lot of odd stares from passers-by. Last held the other end of the rope, ready to pull.

"Give me a hundred heartbeats," she said.

Last snorted. "What am I, a fishmonger with a day–old catch? No bargaining. I'll give you thirty, and I'll pull you out sooner if I see the slidecloth start to shred. You're already going to get your face flayed." Unhappiness weighed down his words.

There was no arguing with him. Short of taking the rope harness off entirely, she couldn't prevent him from yanking her back. Eyo's younger self might have done it in a fit of bravado, but she was smart enough now to accept the precaution. "All right."

She pulled the slidecloth mask down over her face, leaving only her mouth clear. Somehow, not being able to see the storm made it far more frightening. Her pulse pounded, counting off the beats faster than usual. Eyo's breath shallowed, and when she brought the flute to her lips, it took her three tries to produce a sound, even though she'd practiced for this day.

Gevsilon never had much of a breeze, as if the forces that brought Driftwood together needed some cosmic counterbalance for the maelstrom of Oneua. What movement there was died as Eyo began to play, the air settling around her like a warm, damp blanket.

She wasn't ready. But she made herself step forward anyway.

The list of things that didn't work grew longer as the years went by.

Slidecloth didn't last long enough. The flute might have worked, but the winds tore away Eyo's breath before she could produce a note, and when she tried going back with a slidecloth–covered barrel over her head as shelter, the flute only affected the air inside the barrel. Then Uaru had to pick splinters out of her cheek after the barrel shattered. A potion whose seller swore it would make her invulnerable turned out to be nothing more than flavored wine. Someone else legitimately had the ability to turn Eyo insubstantial, but that would have made it impossible for her to do anything else—like carry an object. Burrowing underground kept her safe from the storm; unfortunately, she could spend the rest of her life digging tunnels and never find what she was looking for, not without some way to orient herself. Flying could lift her above the winds, but that didn't change the fact that she would have to descend into them eventually. Remembering her grandparents' stories of how the world dried out before the storm began, Eyo even looked into the possibility of channeling the remnants of the Eckuoz Sea across the border into Oneua, on the principle that it might lay the dust. But a broken dam in Ishlt left the aquatic Leshir in desperate search of a new home, and they took up residence in the waters of Eckuoz before Eyo could put that particular crack–brained idea to the test.

Last showed up intermittently, whenever he found some new prospect for Eyo to consider. Sometimes his absence stretched out to a solar year or more. But she never had any doubt that she would see him again; the possibility of him losing interest was as inconceivable as his death.

He never offered to go into the storm for her. And she never asked.

She worked as a trader, primarily among the Brenak'i, where her scarred face and hand earned her respect. When Eyo was young, the prospect of being a hero to her people had consumed all her thoughts; as the years passed, it slipped further and further into the back of her mind, pushed aside by duties and opportunities more immediate.

But it never went away. And when her daughter was born, it came roaring back to life, as if it had never faded at all.

Ila wasn't her first. Eyo had an older child–pair, a boy and a hanaime, sired by an Oneui lover. But even if her second birth hadn't been single—a rarity among her people—the girl's appearance would have told everyone her father was an outsider, her eyes too small, her face too round, her skin more Brenak'i gold than Oneui red. She had scalp feathers, but none along the backs of her arms.

"It happens with almost everyone, sooner or later," Last said one night. All three of Gevsilon's moons were in the sky, making what the Nigevi had called "false day;" people went about their business in the half–light, but the strip of packed dirt between the tenements and the border was much less busy than usual. "Some peoples manage to keep themselves completely separate until they're gone, and a few seem to be fertile only with their own kind, but most wind up mixing with other races in Drift-wood."

About half the inhabitants of Gevsilon these days were Drifters, the descendants of such cross–world encounters. Products of a hundred worlds, they had no world but Driftwood itself. "It all goes away in the end," Eyo said, her voice thick. "Ila's great–grandchildren will be Drifters. They'll know nothing of Oneua." Then she pounded her fist against the ground. "I say that as if *I* know anything about it. All I know are my grand-parents' stories! I was born after they fled here. We try to live as they did before, but it isn't the same. We eat the food of the Brenak'i, wear fabric the Thiwd make from worms. Without our suns we can't count time correctly, so all our rituals are guesses. If we had—"

She swallowed the words before they could come out. Last nodded. "If you had whatever it is you left behind."

He'd given up on asking her what it was. But he hadn't given up on finding her a way.

Eyo let her head sag. "I know it won't fix anything. Everything in Driftwood fades eventually; the Oneui will be no different. Generations from now, that storm will be gone, and some other dying world will have taken our place. But what happens before then—that still matters. At least to me."

Last stroked her crest. There was no one else she allowed to make such an intimate gesture anymore, now that Uaru had passed away. Last wasn't kin—she didn't even know what world he'd come from—but somewhere during these years of effort, he had become family.

"I'll keep searching," he said. "For you."

Driftwood took, and took, and took—but it also gave.

Ila was growing like a weed and Eyo's eldest pair had passed their rites of adulthood when Last appeared with news from the Edge, the rim of Driftwood where new world fragments appeared. "You have something," Eyo said, hope flaring in her heart.

He'd had something before, countless times. But usually he looked optimistic, or maybe skeptical. This time he looked grim. And that, against all logic, gave her hope.

"I do," Last said, the words dragging with reluctance. "But it—hellfire. Eyo, it's something they do to their *criminals*."

In Driftwood, customs of punishment varied as much as anything else. For all Eyo knew, criminals in this newly-arrived world were made to wear outlandish costumes, or eat foul-smelling herbs. "I don't care. Whatever it is, I'll—"

Last put up his hand before she could finish her sentence. "Don't. I almost didn't even come tell you, except...I can't do that to you. Can't lie. I've always brought you everything, and so I have to bring this. But it's *permanent*, Eyo. Assuming it even works here, you won't be able to come back from it. And I can't swear that it will help you. I don't know what it is you need to retrieve from Oneua, but you might do this to yourself and then find you aren't able to bring that thing out like you want."

"Sa–Last." The formal address brought him up short. Eyo laid her hands over his and said, "Tell me."

He'd lived for a long time. More lifetimes than anyone could count, him included, Eyo thought. Somewhere in all those ages, he'd learned how to spit out bad news without choking on it.

"They turn their criminals into wind."

Her fingers went slack.

Wind.

Like the never–ending storm in Oneua.

"*Self-aware* wind," Last said. "You'll still be yourself. You'll know where you are, and be able to move as you wish. And if what you're looking for is small enough, you might be able to pick it up and blow it to the border. But you'll be like that *forever*, Eyo—until Oneua is gone."

Her heart seemed to have gone silent in her chest. *If what you're looking for is small enough.* It was—oh, it was.

Which meant that if this worked—if these newcomers to Driftwood could change her into wind—if she could find her way into the sanctuary—if she could control herself well enough—

Then she would die. Her mind would linger, but as far as her people were concerned, she would be gone. Lost forever in the storm that had consumed Oneua, until Driftwood finally ground the last of it out of existence.

Eyo said, "Ila is still a child."

Someone else might have thought she was preparing to refuse. But Last knew the Oneui: once Ila passed her rites, Eyo's obligations to her half Brenak'i daughter would be done.

And he knew Eyo.

If the air of Gevsilon hadn't been so still, so quiet, she wouldn't have heard his words. "How long?"

"Two lunar years," Eyo said.

Last nodded. "I'll be ready when the time comes. But if you change your mind—"

They both knew she wouldn't.

No one had come to watch her previous attempts. People who thought they could go back into Oneua were eccentrics at best, lunatics at worst; the polite thing to do was to turn a blind eye.

But when the day came that Eyo faced the border for the final time, the tenements emptied, and the well–trammeled thoroughfare from the dwindling Eckuoz Lake was filled with the silent, watching ranks of Oneui.

Last stood a pace from the border with their visitor, a magistrate from the distant world called Tzuh. If this one was any example, the Tz were a short, stocky people, the least airy beings Eyo could imagine. Last referred to the magistrate as "they," so Eyo thought of them as hanaime, though in truth they had no more gender than a rock—at least that she could see. She hadn't spoken much to them. Right now, all her thoughts were bent on her own people.

The eldest hanaime among them performed the rites: a funeral for one who would soon be dead. Stripped bare, her skin covered in an intricate lace of white paint, Eyo turned to face the border—and was caught halfway through her turn by Ila, flinging her arms around her mother's waist in defiance of all custom.

"I love you," Ila whispered into her shoulder, fierce through the tears. "And I will remember. Every bit of it. I'll teach my children about Oneua, and they will teach theirs, from now until the end of Driftwood."

Eyo laid her cheek atop her daughter's head. The promise was as impossible as it was heartfelt. This was the truth of Driftwood: that in the end, everything went away and was forgotten, no matter how hard people tried to cling to the scraps.

But the effort still meant something.

"Wait for me at the border," Eyo said back, stroking her daughter's crest. "I will bring it to you—I swear."

Then she pried Ila away, gently, and approached Last and the Tz magistrate.

Last met her gaze. *He* understood, she thought. He of all people would.

He murmured a phrase in a language she didn't recognize. His own native tongue? It had the sound of a blessing. Then he stepped back and it was just the magistrate, who set their feet against the ground and began a series of clicking noises that seemed to slip between the pieces that made up Eyo, separating them, slicing the bonds between them until they all came apart—

An instant before she became entirely insubstantial, Last placed his hands against her back and *shoved*.

The storm was never–ending insanity.

Particles of sand tore through Eyo, robbed of their power to harm her. But she cartwheeled through the air without any sense of up or down, left or right; there was only *forward*, borne along on the ever–changing currents. *Backward* did not exist at all. In the face of such fury, even the thought was impossible.

She could not fight the wind, any more than she had been able to withstand it before. In order to survive, she had to join with it. And in order to win passage through, she had to ride the torrent.

Forward, forward, always forward, swirling and veering and tearing across a landscape she knew only from her grand-parents' stories. Everything was worn down by the constant friction of the sand, rounding into smooth shapes she could barely identify. Then it would all vanish, as she arced upward and away and lost track of where she was.

But gradually she learned.

And even more gradually, she began to work her way toward her goal.

It was slow progress. Sometimes she wound up further away than before, her own strength nothing against the power of the storm. But Eyo had learned patience, in her years of trying to enter Oneua. She simply rode the winds away, then came back for another pass. She found spaces between the crumbling build-ings where the fury was quieter. She mapped out the vortices where everything became chaos, and found there was pattern within it after all.

And then, one night when both of Oneua's suns had set, she slipped inside the hollow wreck of a building whose sand–scoured walls still bore the unmistakable tint of green jade.

The winds had broken open doors, windows, roofs. But not floors, not yet—and in here, where only a portion of the storm could reign, Eyo's hard–won skill bore fruit. In a single in-stinctive movement she was across the entry chamber, into the inner room, at the entrance to a spiral staircase winding downward. The storm itself aided her now, dragging her down that spiral, but she almost missed the opening at the bottom, flinging her insubstantial form through it by the narrowest of margins.

Here the air was almost still. The place was as dark as Last's hair; no flame had illuminated it since the Oneui fled. But a wind did not need eyes to see. Eyo spread herself out, floating along at a pace of her own choosing, farther and farther from the reach of the storm. Soon hers was the only movement, drifting past a double rank of statues whose lines were as crisp and unworn as the day they were first carved. They seemed to watch her go by, and Eyo offered up a silent prayer to them, that she would not have done all this in vain.

She had not.

It sat in a shallow bowl of gold, untouched by the distant wind. A single feather: the most holy relic of her people, taken from the crest of Ona, foremother of their race. Too precious and fragile to risk in the storm, the feather had remained behind when the Oneui fled, because they didn't realize they would never be able to return for it.

Eyo could move a feather.

But could she keep it safe from the storm?

She gathered it up with the lightest touch, wafting it on a breath of air to the center of herself. She would have only one opportunity: once she re–entered the tempest, there would be no chance to retreat and try again. If she lost control of the feather, or let the sand rip through her and her precious burden . . .

Waiting would not make her any more ready. Eyo wrapped herself around the feather, prayed, and launched herself back into the wind.

A balcony lined the back wall of the Oneui settlement in Gevsilon, facing the border.

Children played there in their idle moments, and laundry often hung from its railing. Still, the place had a touch of the sacred to it, and from time to time anyone who came out there would pause in their work or play and gaze at the border with Oneua, the unabated fury of the storm just a short distance away. Moss and flowers grew in the space between, since the thoroughfare had been blocked up.

Ila sat in her accustomed spot just a pace away from that silent, sand–torn barrier. Waiting.

A bell rang, near the center of Gevsilon. She'd grown accustomed to the sound since the Wilsl moved in, taking the place of the now–extinct Nigevi. Soon one of the children would bring her food, and brush her hair, and talk with her for a little while before leaving her to her vigil.

She never troubled herself to wonder what would happen after she was gone. Her mother had promised to bring the feather to her. Ila's faith was absolute.

Something swirled by in the sand and was gone.

Ila rose, so quickly her aging bones protested. Had she imagined it...?

Then it came again. Without hesitation, she plunged her hand through the intangible barrier, from one world into the next, and took hold of what she'd seen.

She expected to feel sand tear the skin from her hand, the flesh from her bones. Instead she felt a brief, soft caress—and then, before the storm could take her, Ila pulled her hand back.

Slowly, not daring to breathe, she uncurled her fingers. Ona's crest feather balanced in her palm, iridescent and gold.

Tears slipped down Ila's cheeks. "Thank you," she whispered to the storm, then turned to face the Oneui who had come to a halt on the balcony, raising the feather high above her head.

Eyo had kept her promise.

"*Help me*. Please. Don't let them make *more* of me!
Don't let them make the world worse than it already *is*."
Pat McEwen

The Forever Boy

Patricia MacEwen

Tsula was asleep on her feet, held upright by the crush of other people around her. She woke with a start as a shudder wracked the body pressed up against her back. She heard her mother moan a single hopeless word, almost a prayer. "*No.*"

Then water splashed down her bare legs, warm as urine but stickier.

Tsula pushed against everyone else enough that she was able to turn around, but that was all she could do. That and try to wrap her arms around her mother's quaking figure. That embrace let her feel it when the next ripple passed through the muscles in her mother's swollen belly.

That's when she knew what was happening. She was ten years old, and raised on a farm, after all. Tsula felt her heart leap with pure panic.

"Help us!" she begged of the people surrounding them. "Please!" she cried. "We've got to make room. My mother's having a baby!"

There was no room to make. The night before, on arriving here, they'd been jammed into this stadium by men with dead eyes, dogs, and automatic rifles. They'd been forced to fill every inch of the space. They had no water, no shade, no food, and the heat of so many people, pressed together, was growing unbearable.

There was nowhere to go. There was only the stadium's PA system, making yet another useless announcement: "Your attention, please. The convoy bringing bottled water, emergency rations, and blankets is now expected to arrive at thirteen hundred hours. Please keep calm and help us maintain order. Your patience is appreciated."

Tsula tried again. "We need help. *Please!*" She screamed the words this time.

A few of those closest to her tried to make way, enough so her mother could lie down at least. It didn't work. Within seconds, those further away began pushing back and the sliver of space disappeared. Then there were hands, though, many hands, reaching out to her mother, taking hold of her wrists, her arms, her dress, and even her braided hair. They were holding her up, Tsula realized. Assisting her in the only way they could.

They should have stayed in Chickasha. But when their hoard of food ran out, they'd headed north up I-44 toward Oklahoma City, on foot like everyone else. And got just about halfway there, she figured, before running into the National Guard.

Tsula remembered being so happy to see them.

The soldiers, though, hadn't tried to help anyone on the road. They'd been shunted off onto a county road and then into the Gaylord Family Oklahoma Memorial Stadium. Home of the Sooners. Where the Guard was going to do... what?

Maybe nothing, she thought, and was even more frightened by that prospect. Nothing meant no water. No food. No shelter. No hope.

Her mother wailed as a fresh contraction seized her.

"Help us!" Tsula cried. To the sky, this time.

"What is that *smell?*" Dustu paused in the middle of the game, having caught the small deer-hide ball in the cup on the end of his stick. "Is there a feedlot around here?"

His opponent was full-grown but still only waist-high to Dustu, who stood just a bit more than four feet tall. Uncle shrugged as he sniffed the fetid air. "It's not cattle."

"Then what?"

"Human things."

Feedlots were human things—places where cattle were penned up in muck of their own making, fed grain instead of good grass, and never ever given any room to run. Never a chance to play. To live. To be anything but a rump roast on four feet.

It was all part of the wrong-thinking thing, where machines and gasoline somehow got to be more important than life itself, than taking care of the earth.

"Ha!" Somebody's stick swept around his knees and then upward to whack his wrist, hard. The ball went flying. A second player on the Eastern team struck out with his own stick, failing to catch the ball but propelling it downfield. The rest of the Little People galloped past in hot pursuit.

"No fair!" Dustu hollered, dropping his stick to cradle his suddenly useless forearm.

"It's *anetsa!*" cried Uncle. "There are no rules to break, boy!"

Before he could even reply, a complex three-part relay conveyed the small ball to the end of the meadow and through the gap between two saplings they'd cut down and stuck in the ground to serve as goalposts. The saplings, of course, were only a few inches taller than Dustu himself. The *Yunwi Tsunsdi* didn't build much of anything human-scale in size.

Dustu frowned, testing his wrist. The aroma grew stronger. They were downwind of... what? Oh. The big football stadium, where humans were apt to play far tamer games and wear all sorts of padding and helmets instead of a good coat of bear grease.

"Play!" cried a team-mate, racing past him as he stood there, but Dustu held up his arm. "I'm out. It's broken."

"Then play with the other hand!" Uncle shouted, flinging his long glossy hair back over his shoulder, hair almost as long as his own small body.

"You know it takes me longer to heal than you do," Dustu answered. He turned away just as another louder crack split the air, and his heart as well. Gunshot! It came from the stadium. *What on earth?* he asked himself, and was seized by a memory. Long ago. Somebody running. Running away from the Trail of Tears, trying for the trees, for a chance at freedom. A girl his own age back then, nine or ten. And the bluecoat raising his rifle. One sharp crack, just like that one, had sent the runner tumbling into a creek, half her head gone. For no other reason than she was a Cherokee who didn't want to leave home.

Sickness stirred in his middle. That feeling of helpless rage again.

Dustu swallowed it, buried it in that armored place underneath his heart as he took his playing sticks off the field and laid them down by his other gear. Uncle strode toward him.

"Is *that* all it takes to stop you, boy?"

No, but the sudden onslaught of memory, of nausea, was another matter. Uncle sighed, took hold of his bad hand and pulled it outward. Something grated in his arm as the broken bits of bone popped into alignment again. Dustu hissed like a snake, and then the pain died rapidly as Uncle held onto that hand and chanted a healing song he'd first heard on a mountain bald near Nikwasi. The whites now called that whole area North Carolina.

When it was done, the forearm felt tender and fragile. The purplish-black bruise, however, was already fading. A week should see it whole again, as strong as ever.

"Many thanks, Uncle." Then, using mainly his left hand, he picked up his knife belt and gingerly tied it on over his loincloth.

Uncle raised an eyebrow.

"I'm going to find out what smells so bad."

Darkness gleamed in the little man's eyes as his usual wry grin disappeared. "Are you sure you want to know?"

Dustu frowned, then nodded decisively. Better to know than wonder, stomach churning as he remembered more and more of his days on the Trail.

"Then maybe I'd better go with you."

Tsula stared at the broken doll-shape that hung from the coils of razor wire topping the fence along the end zone. The sheer wrongness kept her from seeing what it really was for a minute or more—a body. A barefoot man who'd suddenly run at the fence and started to climb it with just his fingers and toes, screaming something in Spanish about water.

Somebody cried out, "They *shot* him."

An answering wave of voices melded into a roar. People surged toward the fences. Some fought for handholds, attempting to climb it like the first man had, the one now hanging upside down, blood running down both arms. So wrong, that vivid crimson, when everything else was shades of brown. There'd been no water to spare for bathing, for laundry, for months now. Most people wore what they had 'til it fell apart, then stole something newer and cleaner, or else went without in the dry heat gripping the whole Midwest.

More gunshots, fired into the air this time, but the would-be climbers got the message and fell back, rejoining the masses on the playing field.

"Do not attempt to climb the barriers," bellowed the PA. "For your own safety. Keep calm and stay where you are. Assistance is on the way,"

But why were they being confined on the field in the first place? Why keep them so jam-packed? The man with the mike was lying to all of them. Why? What were they really intending to do?

Tsula heard a godawful shrieking from her mother. She fought the crush, turning back to her by jumping upward and pulling on random arms, on clothing. She was just in time to see the raw terror in her mother's face. See the fresh wave of agony roll through her body. Hear the wet splat from down below.

There wasn't time to think.

Tsula dove downward, swimming through body parts like they were snags in the Washita River. She followed her mother's bloody legs down into the depths. There, she put two fingertips on a small form, caught hold of a tiny limb and forced herself upward again, with the baby in tow.

Dustu's stomach wasn't happy. The smell just got worse and worse and the air was thick with bluebottle flies, like something had died. Something big.

There were soldiers all over the place.

Too quiet, too, he thought. Nobody here was joking around, just mumbling stuff as they huddled underneath what was left of the shade trees and sucked on their beer cans. More than a few were sharing needles, cooking something in teaspoons with cigarette lighters and then injecting each other. He was glad they couldn't see or hear him while he was with Uncle.

There were more soldiers guarding the gates and the ticket booths at the main entrance. So he and Uncle walked around the side until they found a service entrance. There, two big semis were backed up to a loading dock, disgorging enormous wooden crates. More soldiers were passing out the contents to their compadres—spray guns with hoses and weird bug-faced mask things and rubbery yellow suits and boots.

"Move it along, boys," a grizzled sergeant was telling the men. "All be over soon. This here is just another clean-up detail."

Dustu shot a puzzled look at Uncle, but the *yvwi usdi* pointed at a freight elevator almost full of yellow-suited soldiers, the bug-eyed things hanging from straps around their necks. The two of them slipped inside just as the doors closed.

One of the soldiers, a skinny gink with a big Adam's apple, aimed a finger at one of the spray guns held by an older man. "Does that shit work?

"Sure. Takes a while, but it does the job. It's like sprayin' for roaches. You lay it down good and thick. Wait twenty minutes and bing bang bong—you're done."

Dustu recoiled. The man reeked of cheap whiskey and too little soap. Long ago, there'd been another who smelled like that, who used that tone. "Lice. That's all they are," said the bleary-eyed bluecoat attempting to button up his trousers. "Just pop 'em between your fingernails and move on, son. Ain't no point to buryin' *that*." He waved a careless dirt-crusted hand at Dustu's sister where she lay naked in the dirt, legs splayed. So vivid was the memory that Dustu jumped when the older man in the here and now smacked the new guy's arm. "If you're gonna be sick, boy, don't ralph on *my* boots."

"I'm not! I'm... okay. I just didn't know it would s*tink* like this."

That got a laugh from a couple of others. "We gotta clean up this shit," one of them told him. "Whole damn country's gonna smell better when we're done."

Dustu's hand landed on the hilt of his knife, but Uncle took hold of his wrist and shook his head, long black hair glimmering in the artificial light. They rode the rest of the way to the top in silence.

Tsula surfaced with the baby. It was white underneath all the blood and muck and waxy stuff. So white. Translucent. Like a Christmas tree angel. The purple birth cord still hung from its belly, and it wasn't crying at all. Not breathing.

"*What do I do?*" Tsula cried.

"Give it here," said an old black man. He took the limp form, cradled it in one arm and hooked a filthy forefinger into the baby's mouth, clearing out a wad of mucus. Then he compressed the baby's chest with the palm of his hand, five times, quickly and gently. He bent to press his mouth down around the lower half of the baby's face, nose and all. He puffed a breath in once, twice, and then went back to the chest compressions.

Tsula prayed. To Selu, the Corn Mother, first. Then Water Beetle, who made the Earth and gave birth to all people back in the very beginning. And finally Jesus, just in case Aunt Inola was wrong about him.

At length, the old man shook his head. "Sorry," he told Tsula. "That's all I know how to do."

He handed the baby back to her but Tsula's mother surged forward and snatched the small body right out of her hands. She held the limp infant against her chest and burst into tears as she rocked him back and forth, still being held upright by everyone else. In her mother's face, there was no sign of recognition even when she looked straight at Tsula. Something was gone. Broken.

Tsula shivered, afraid as she'd never been before. Even when she'd found her Dad and finally understood why he never came home that day.

She grabbed hold of other people and pulled herself up on top of them. She began swimming across the sea of sunburnt heads and bent necks and bowed shoulders. Kicking off against them, she groped for new hand holds in hair, collars, anything at all. She would *find* a way out. She'd get help for her Mom, or die trying.

"Uncle, we *have* to do something," Dustu said as they emerged into glaring sunlight along the outer wall of the stadium.

"Do we?"

Dustu stared at the *yvwi usdi*, reminded once again. He was human. The Little People weren't. And they might have helped him, even taken him in, but they didn't take sides in human quarrels. Even so...

"It's not right," he insisted, heading across the vaulted roof.

"Nothing human is. Blame Water Beetle for that. He was in such a hurry, he made you too quickly. That's why you're all a little crooked inside."

They climbed up another ladder to the top of the sky boxes. Up here, it smelled a lot better thanks to the ever-present prairie wind but now he could hear the mass misery rising from all the people trapped below, like the earth itself was moaning in black despair.

A sound he'd long forgotten. Now it clutched at his gut.

All these soldiers, he thought. All these guns, more deadly than anything the bluecoats ever had back then, when they uprooted everyone and began herding his people west.

Uncle canted his head as he studied Dustu. "This is not a fight one man can win."

And he wasn't a man, was he? Dustu hadn't grown a single inch in those two hundred years since he ran away into the wilderness and the Little People found him. For the first time, Dustu wished he *was* taller. Meaner. More lethal. So he could take out every one of these whiter than white bastards wearing the arm bands.

He should have remembered how it was that the Little People found him. That they could hear wishes and unspoken prayers. They could feel human terror and yearning and grief.

"You are on the wrong track," Uncle said, frowning. "If they kill your people for being Red, and you kill theirs for being White, how are you any different from them?"

"How else am I gonna stop them?" Dustu demanded, refusing to back down this time around, the way he always had before.

He got no answer. But that was the way of the Little People, wasn't it? They didn't change. And they didn't jump in. Didn't try to change others or alter the course of events. Their advice was always the same: Don't take life too seriously. Don't worry so much. Don't work so hard. Have fun whenever you can.

They never change. *Is it because they can't*, he thought? *Or won't?* They act like *they're* kids too. Like nothing is up to them. Like dancing and singing and playing tricks on other folks is all that really matters.

Tricks. Realization hit like a thunderbolt.

Dustu turned back to Uncle. "We're Laurel Clan," Dustu said carefully. "Not Rock. Not Tree or Dogwood."

"That's true." Uncle nodded.

"Rock Clan would punish them."

"If they did bad things to Rock Clan," said Uncle. "Invaded their places. Cut down *their* trees. Stripped the tops off *their* mountains. Hurt *them*."

"And Dogwood Clan—they'd try to help those people, if they could, but they wouldn't fight bluecoats."

"It's not the way of the Yunwi Tsunsdi. Especially not Dogwood Clan."

"But... what if we *don't* go to war. What if..." The idea was unfolding inside his head so fast he couldn't quite find the words to keep up with it.

Uncle could, though, and after a minute or two his gaze softened. He started to smile. "You're right," he told Dustu. "That *is* the way of the *Yunwi Tsunsdi*."

He took a deep breath to steady himself, then urged Uncle, "So call them together."

"I have already done so."

Dustu looked down at the parking lots surrounding the stadium. He could see them emerging. Hundreds of Little People popped into plain view, emerging from reflections off car windows, or any bright glint of light. They stared up at him. Waiting.

Tsula finally reached the sidelines, where people were pleading with the soldiers on the other side of the fence. "Water!" most of them cried. Or a simple, "Help!"

More soldiers appeared, but these men wore bright yellow coveralls. What were they doing? They had a bunch of pallet jacks, each one loaded with big steel barrels of something or other.

Dustu shook his head, backing away from Uncle. "*Me?* I can't!"

"It is not my place to speak *for* you," said the little man. "Those are your people, and this is your idea."

"But they're not my people." *You are,* he didn't say. Mostly because it no longer felt totally true. Inside, something had changed. And the people down there on the field—there were plenty of Cherokee, sure. Shawnee too, and Chickasaw. Creeks and Wyandottes. Caddoes and Wichitas. Other folks were black. And a lot of them looked like they might be Asian or Indian or Mexican or whatever mixed in with white or with something else. But they weren't *his* people, any of them, because *they* had all died two hundred years back, even if they survived the Trail of Tears.

"This matters to *you*," Uncle told him. "Stand up. Speak your piece."

Dustu could not run away. Not this time. So he pulled himself as erect as he could and swallowed the lump in his throat.

Trusting Uncle to make sure all the *Yunwi Tsunsdi* could hear him, and nobody else, he forced his first words out. No plan to it. Just whatever boiled up from the place where his heart had been.

Tsula was reaching for the fence herself, ready to try and scramble up over it on her own, anything to get help for her mother. Or an answer. Or a drink of water. That's when she heard it. A boy's voice, not a man's this time. And not on the PA system either, but almost as loud.

"Look, I love you," he said. "I always have. Being one of you— that's all I've wanted for *so* long. You saved my life. You saved *me*. I'll never forget that.

Where was he? *Who* was he? Who was he talking to?

"But if we don't do something, right now, then terrible things are going to happen. Just like it did before. Only this time? It's going to be worse. So much worse. I need your help. Help me stop it. This piece of it, anyway. I know you can't do what we do. The human thing. That's okay."

Human thing?

Who was he talking to?

"You can be you, though," the boy went on. "That's what I'm asking for. Do what we've..." He paused, "What you've always done. Make trouble. Play your tricks. Mess it up, whatever they try to do."

Tricks? What did he mean by that? Or was *she* going crazy? The boy's tone changed. She heard tears in his voice now. Agony as he pleaded with somebody.

"*Help me.* Please. Don't let them make *more* of me! Don't let them make the world worse than it already *is*."

There was nothing else in him, so Dustu stopped talking. He waited, his face wet with sweat, his throat sore. Eventually, he sneaked a sideways glance at Uncle.

"Did they hear me?"

His answer did not come from Uncle. Down below, something exploded. A reddish white cloud of ash or smoke shot up from the center of one yellow spiderweb. Whatever that was, it hit guardsmen who were not wearing the bunny suits. All of a sudden, there were angry voices shouting all sorts of things and the soldiers without yellow suits started running up the stairs in that section, hell-bent on escaping whatever it was.

On the other side of the stadium, a barrel rolled into some of the soldiers and knocked them flat. A couple of soldiers got squashed. The bright yellow hoses they'd been stretching out toward their targets abruptly came to life. Some wrapped themselves around anyone nearby—hands, arms, legs or necks. Some guns either smacked soldiers across the face or rammed themselves into any open mouth as the owner screamed. Others reared up into the air and sprayed the soldiers all on their own, with that very same reddish-brown powdery stuff that had panicked the first bunch.

From there, it was chaos. The crackle of gunfire erupted as those being sprayed with that shit turned their guns on the guys in the bunny suits.

All of a sudden, the whole place roared.

It was the crowd trapped inside the fence.

Yes!

Sensing a chance that might not come again, they let loose all of *their* anger. They started boosting each other up onto their knees, then their shoulders, their heads even. Human surf surged upward, over the tops of the fences, collapsing them onto the soldiers. Then masses of people burst free of the field and more guardsmen went down under thousands of filthy feet.

It took only seconds, however, for more of the guardsmen to make an appearance at higher levels. To start shooting at the escapees.

Just like the bluecoats.

A cold rage ripped through him. Dustu ran for the ladder they'd climbed to get up there, not caring what Uncle might think or do.

Crack! Crack! Crack!

Tsula fell flat, landing in between the seats as a guardsman appeared at the top of the section she was climbing and started spraying the people just ahead of her with an automatic rifle. He didn't seem to care that he was hitting some of his own in the process while they struggled with the climbers. There was a blaze of madness in his blue eyes.

Someone screeched as they toppled over. A woman. She landed on top of Tsula's legs, blood spurting out of her in hot pulses 'til she gave a couple of twitches and went totally still.

Tsula crammed her fist into her mouth to keep from screaming about that. Play dead, she told herself, knowing it wouldn't work.

Dustu plunged through the big square doorway and into the dazzle of sunlight. Half blinded, he couldn't hear anything but the gun going off *rat-a-tat* some fifteen rows down and off to his left.

The man firing that rifle was laughing hysterically as he went down the steps one by one. He just kept right on shooting, mowing down people in great bloody swathes.

It took no thought at all to decide what to do. Dustu pulled his knife free of its sheath and leaped like a deer down the rows of seats, taking two at a time. Didn't matter how much of a ruckus he made. Couldn't hear it himself, over everything else, so the laughing soldier had no clue what was happening. Not 'til he buried the knife in the soldier's back.

The man spun, trying to bring his gun to bear on Dustu, but a girl reached up from behind him to haul on his rifle's strap. When he toppled backward over the seat, she bent over him and pulled a bayonet from a sheath at the soldier's waist. With a glittering sloe-eyed glance up at Dustu, she used it to cut the man's throat.

Rising, she stared at Dustu, then shifted her gaze to something behind him. Another soldier? He whipped around, knife ready.

No. It was Uncle.

"Who are *you*?" she demanded.

The little man was beautiful—a knee-high boy doll in beaded leather leggings and moccasins. He was perfect in every dimension. Especially all that glossy black hair, falling down to his ankles. Just for a moment, Tsula could imagine a little hairbrush in her own hand...

Then he moved. He stepped forward into the sunlight and spoke to the boy in Cherokee. She caught a couple words. Most of it—no.

The boy answered in the same language, and she caught more, but that's when Tsula realized he was wearing an actual breech clout instead of shorts. Moccasins too, and a feather in his hair. Like a picture in a history book.

The boy stared back at her, then asked, "How come she can see me? How can she see *you*?"

The little man shrugged. "It's only twins can see us, easy. If we don't want them to, nobody can."

Tsula frowned and stumbled over some of the words as she said, "I—I had a twin. She died before I was born." Something happened with the birth cord. They should have done a C-section but there was no doctor anymore at the tribal clinic. She'd heard her mother tell Aunt Inola that late one night, the two of them drinking the last of the beer and crying about it when they thought Tsula was fast asleep.

Tsula spun around toward the playing field. Where *was* her Mom?

"What..." Dustu started to say, but a fresh burst of gunfire cut him short. There were firefights going on all over the stadium now as escapees took up fallen soldiers' weapons and turned them against anyone in a uniform.

There weren't enough ways for the prisoners to get out of the stadium. Too many exits had been blocked off.

"How are we going to get them all out?" he asked Uncle.

"We? They'll find their own way, given time."

But there wasn't going to be time. At his back, Dustu felt a weird pounding sensation, a thudding heartbeat. He looked up to see a black helicopter swoop down out of the sky. It was coming right at him, it seemed like, so he ducked back into the entrance to the hallway behind him. The girl did too, bayonet ready, and Uncle as well.

Once it dropped inside the bowl of the stadium, cannons on the front end of the copter cut loose, spinning like mad as they spat bullets everywhere. The sound of it was ungodly, and the bullets tore people apart by the dozens who were still trying to get off the field. Their screams of fright and despair cut a hole through his heart.

"Mom!" the girl cried, although it was surely impossible to make out individuals in all that.

"What do we do?" Dustu cried out, but if Uncle answered, he couldn't hear it over all the fresh uproar. And then, as the heartbeat outside of him got complicated, two more of the ugly machines dropped out of the sky.

There was no way to stop them that he could see. Not with a knife. Even the rifles the soldiers had were no match for those things. But as he stared upward, the light changed again. A big gray thunderhead had been blown between him and the sun, casting shade over more than a third of the stadium, and it wasn't the only one up there.

Where had they come from? Was a storm blowing in?

Dustu's jaw dropped. The Thunder Boys? Had *they* heard him? He turned his head Uncle's way.

"They heard *her*," said the little man, nodding toward the girl.

Hope blossomed, even in the dead place under his heart. "Can we..."

Uncle's gaze stopped him. "You know what they're like," said the *yvwi usdi*.

"But they *live* in the sky! They can reach those bastards!"

"The *Asagaya Gigaei* do nothing by half measures. If you call *them* down, there's no telling how much destruction will follow."

"But if we don't..."

He couldn't finish the sentence. He knew what Uncle meant. People would die. On both sides of it. He would be striking down some of his own, too, in trying to save the rest. There'd be no way to choose who would live, who would die.

"It is not a decision a *boy* can make," Uncle told him.

Dustu felt that painful lump reappear in his throat, and the girl's gaze scalded him. "What are you talking about?" she demanded. "The thunder boys? They're just an old story."

"Really," said Uncle, amused for an instant, not bothering even to point out the obvious.

"Oh! I..." The girl's far-too-thin face flooded with color, but she held her ground. "My Mom is down there."

But there was no other way. Lose some or lose all. That was the choice he had to make. *No! Run away!* said part of him. Run and hide! It was small though, compared to the things he had already done today. He'd made himself see this. He'd forced himself to do something about it, to stand up in front of his people—his adopted people, he thought, correcting himself with a tiny judder of shame and surprised regret– and he'd asked for their help with it. He'd killed a man. There was already blood on his hands. On his knife.

"I know," he told both of them.

Uncle examined him one more time but a glimmer of sadness in his dark eyes was his only objection. "You'll need to call on the female force too," was all he said.

Female rain came from the south, the gentle kind that nurtured the crops and filled the rain barrels without the rivers running wild. It was the kind the *Asagaya Gigaei* had brought them for two hundred years now, ever since the Cherokee were driven down out of the mountains and across the Mississippi. Women were the source of true power. Of life itself.

He turned to the girl. "Do you know the Green Corn Dance?"

Tsula's heart sank. She wanted to fly down the steps to the playing field, to find her mother, to take shelter in her Mom's arms and feel safe again just for a minute.

"If we can save *anybody*," the boy whispered, "we have to do that."

He was right. Slowly, she nodded. She moved to stand at his side. She spread out the bottom edge of her dirty t-shirt in place of the apron she didn't have. The little man produced a dried snake's rattle. He shook that instead of the usual kind and started to sing as the two of them took their first hesitant steps in a circle around him.

Dustu bent over. With every fifth step, he spread his hands and then swept them together, scooping up imaginary corn from the concrete. He pretended to pour it all into the girl's t-shirt. "Bring us rain," Uncle sang, adding lines that weren't part of the dance. "Bring us water. Bring us life!"

The corn wouldn't happen without them. Without corn, the people would disappear. Those who weren't mowed down would starve. They were already starving. Dustu's anger returned, and the rhythm of the dance and the song changed. Became louder. Faster. The quiet careful steps turned into a stomping progression and somehow his knife had jumped into his hand again. He began grunting as he swung the knife at the enemy he could now see in his mind's eye. Beside him, the girl was still holding her shirt out on one side, but she had that bayonet. She made the same chopping moves with it. They had no war clubs to swing, but soon they were both howling a full-throated war cry, in unison.

Their answer came in the form of a distant flicker of brightness, a buffet of wind. Then more clouds. A gathering darkness that plunged everything into shadow.

The storm cloud above them had changed its contours too. It was bigger by far and part of it was angular now. Anvil-shaped. And the wind was still picking up speed.

Lightning flashed, not a glimmer this time but a blast of light, and thunder crashed almost on top of it, louder than even the guns and choppers.

He danced harder, faster, the girl matching every step. "They've killed the corn," she cried suddenly. "They've killed the rain! They've killed my baby brother!"

"They're going to kill *all* the babies!" he shouted, remembering how many died on the Trail and how many were never born. "They want to *end* us!"

The sky roared in outrage. Wind suddenly gathered its strength and struck them like fists, and then came hailstones. Small ones at first, cold as death, needle sharp. Then came big ones, apple-sized, hitting the seats and the stairways like ice bombs, shattering, flinging shrapnel every which way. They ran for the shelter of reinforced concrete, where the girl clung to Dustu as one, two, *three!* funnel clouds dropped down out of the madness above to hit the first helicopter and then the playing field and the stands.

Something flashed, blindingly bright, and the 'copter jinked sideways. It kept right on firing but didn't recover. It rolled in the air, turning over and over until it came low enough, its rotors hit iron railings. A terrible clanging sent chunks of it scything across the stadium. Then the rest of it dropped straight down to explode in flames where it hit the ground.

One of the funnels pulled people right off the ground, and then barrels and hoses off the stands. All that whirled upward and over the sky boxes, out of sight.

The third funnel spun around inside the stadium, sweeping across the different seating levels and scrubbing them like a gigantic whirling toilet brush. Debris made it hard to see anything, let alone who was hit, who'd been taken, or even what side anybody was on.

All the noise was now due to the *Asagaya Gigaei* and not guns. A hard pelting male rain struck, replacing the hail, and he couldn't see anything anymore. He buried his face in the girl's dark hair as they retreated further into the depths of the stadium. He kept his arms wrapped around her, his head bent over hers, trying to shield her. All the while, Uncle clung to his left leg.

It's over, Tsula told herself.

She wasn't sure she believed it. The rain was still coming down, heavy as hell, and the sky was still dark, but the lightning had stopped and the thunder along with it. Everything, now, was wet and quiet.

She disentangled herself from the boy and stepped back. Was he taller now?

"I don't even know your name," she said.

"Dustu."

The little green tree frog? A boy's name, she thought. Not a man's. And then, as she remembered the stories Uncle Adahy used to tell, she felt her jaw drop. "You...you're the Forever Boy?"

He didn't know how to answer that. To most people it meant the boy who refused to grow up. Peter Pan. Not the boy whose home and family and childhood were stolen.

Uncle stepped in. "No, Dustu. You're not a boy. Not anymore. You are neither one children, not after this." He waved a hand at the half-gutted stadium.

Hundreds of bodies lay scattered amidst the filth and the wreckage. Yet thousands more huddled together against the rain, supporting each other and swallowing what they could as it ran down their faces and washed them clean. Not exactly his people, thought Dustu, but close enough. For one thing, there wasn't a single soldier still upright among them.

"Go," Uncle said.

"But...where?" Dustu asked him.

"Go north. Take your people and find a new place where there's still water. Rebuild the world so we all have a place in it."

"I'm afraid," Dustu admitted.

"Of course," said Uncle. "You're not a fool." Then he looked at the girl. "And you're not alone."

She shot a dark questioning look his way. Dustu shrugged.

That's when she told him, "My name is Tsula."

"Frog and Fox!" Uncle laughed. "Now that is a strong combination."

I curse the wall.
Jane Yolen

This Desert Is the Place

JANE YOLEN

This desert is the place
where once my heart lived,
then a prairie, a meadow,
a sanctuary for bees.

Children played in the shadows
of trees. Otters poked
their grey curious noses
out of the river.

A solitary fox often trotted by.

If we shiver—though once
it was only in the cold
of January—now January
is all the years.

My grandchildren are warriors,
or in warrens, being re-educated,
with flowing tears. I am not
near enough to hold them.

The only spectrum now is that of color.

I lift the hijab of longing,
Place it on my shoulders,
not my head. The lectern
of learning is in shards.

What is there to do but die
a little at a time, for guns,
knives are forbidden us.
It will be a long hard death.

I curse the wall.

About the Contributors

Aliette de Bodard lives and works in Paris. She is the author of the critically acclaimed Obsidian and Blood trilogy of Aztec noir fantasies, as well as numerous short stories which have garnered her two Nebula Awards, a Locus Award and two British Science Fiction Association Awards. Her space opera books include *The Citadel of Weeping Pearls*, a book set in the same universe as her Vietnamese science fiction *On a Red Station Drifting*. Recent works include the Dominion of the Fallen series, set in a turn-of-the-century Paris devastated by a magical war, which comprises *The House of Shattered Wings* (Roc/Gollancz, 2015 British Science Fiction Association Award, Locus Award finalist), and its standalone sequel *The House of Binding Thorns* (Ace, Gollancz).

Seanan McGuire lives and writes in the Pacific Northwest, where she shares her home with her enormous fluffy cats, large collection of creepy dolls, and more books than she can read in her estimated remaining lifetime. This does not stop her from obtaining more.

Seanan can be found on Twitter at @seananmcguire, or at www.seananmcguire.com.

Irene Radford has been writing stories ever since she figured out what a pencil was for. Editing grew out of her love of the craft of writing. Mostly Irene writes fantasy and historical fantasy including the best-selling *Dragon Nimbus* Series and the masterwork *Merlin's Descendants* series. In other lifetimes she writes urban fantasy as P.R. Frost or Phyllis Ames, and space opera as C.F. Bentley. Lately she ventured into Steampunk as Julia Verne

St. John. If you wish information on the latest releases from Ms. Radford, under any of her pen names, you can subscribe to her newsletter: www.ireneradford.net of subscribe to her Patreon Account https://www.patreon.com/user?u=5806073

Gregory L. Norris is a full-time professional writer, with work appearing in numerous short story anthologies, national magazines, novels, the occasional TV episode, and, so far, one produced feature film (Brutal Colors, which debuted on Amazon Prime January 2016). A former feature writer and columnist at Sci Fi, the official magazine of the Sci Fi Channel (before all those ridiculous Ys invaded), he once worked as a screenwriter on two episodes of Paramount's modern classic, Star Trek: Voyager. Two of his paranormal novels (written under his rom-de-plume, Jo Atkinson, were published by Home Shopping Network as part of their "Escape With Romance" line— the first time HSN has offered novels to their global customer base. He judged the 2012 Lambda Awards in the SF/F/H category. Three times now, his stories have notcheHonorable Mentions in Ellen Datlow's Best-of books. In May 2016, he traveled to Hollywood to accept HM in the Roswell Awards in Short SF Writing. Follow his literary adventures at www.gregorylnorris.blogspot.com.

Brenda Cooper's recent novels include Wilders (Pyr, 2017) POST (*Espec Books, 2016*), Edge of Dark (*Pyr, 2015*), and Spear of Light* (Pyr, 2016).* Brenda blogs frequently on envi-ronmental and futurist topics, and her non-fiction has appeared in *Slate* and *Crosscut*.

She is the winner of the 2007 and 2016 Endeavor Awards for "a distinguished science fiction or fantasy book written by a Pacific Northwest author or authors." Her work has also been nominated for the Phillip K. Dick and Canopus awards.

Learn more or sign up for her mailing list at her website: http://www.brenda-cooper.com.

Joyce Reynolds-Ward is a writer, horsewoman, former middle school learning specialist, and skier splitting her time between Portland and Enterprise, Oregon. Besides earning a SemiFinalist placement in Writers of the Future, she's had short stories and essays published in *Random Realities, M-Brane SF, Zombiefied, River, Gears and Levers 1, How Beer Saved the World, Trust and Treachery, Fantasy Scroll Magazine*, and many other venues. She has also written a number of novels - science ficiton in *The Netwalk Sequence* (*Life in the Shadows:Diana and Will, Netwalk: Expanded Edition, Netwalker Uprising,Netwalk's Children* and *Netwalking Space*) high fantasy (with a non-European setting) in *Goddess's Honor (Beyond Honor (prequel),Pledges of Honor* and *Challenges to Honor*), and standalone *Seeking Shelter at the End of the World* (a cozy apocalypse). When not teaching, she's often thundering about on her intrepid reining mare Mocha, living la vida ski bum, and writing.

Follow Joyce's adventures through her blog, Peak Amygdala, at www.joycereynoldsward.com.

Brooklyn-based author and journalist **Randee Dawn** published her collection of dark speculative fiction short stories, "Home for the Holidays" in 2014, and in 2009 co-authored "The Law & Order: SVU Unofficial Companion". Her short fiction has appeared in 3AM Magazine, Well-Told Tales and Fantasia Divinity. Characters from her story in this anthology ("Can't Find My Way Home") appear in her first novel, "Leave No Trace", which is seeking publication and is represented by Dunham Literary. She can be found at randeedawn.com and @randeedawn on Twitter.

Jacey Bedford is a British writer, published by DAW in the USA. She writes both science fiction and fantasy. Her *Psi-Tech* space opera trilogy consists of *Empire of Dust, Crossways*, and *Nimbus*. Her historical fantasy *Rowankind* trilogy is 2/3 complete with *Winterwood* and *Silverwolf*. Expect the third instalment soon.Her short stories have been published in anthologies and magazines, and translated into an odd assortment of languages including Estonian, Galician and Polish. She's been a folk singer with vocal trio, Artisan, and her claim to fame is singing live on BBC Radio4 accompanied by the Doctor (Who?) playing spoons. More at www.jaceybedford.co.uk

Alma Alexander appears here by gracious permission of the other authors gathered here—with a topical reprint story nominated (upon initial publication) for the Pushcart Prize. She also functions as the editor and the anthologist of this collection, one of her proudest accomplishments. She is the author of a number of novels, internationally published in more than 14 languages, and you can learn more about her at her website (www.AlmaAlexander.org).

Nora Saroyan does not have an Internet presence—she doesn't do social media and so far a professional site has not been required since the story in this anthology is her first actual story sale. She is not, herself, a direct refugee—but she is a first-generation immigrant, and she has family who have been refugees in the past. She wishes to express her gratitude to anyone who purchases and reads this collection—in the name of all those people who stand to be helped through its existence, and in whose multitudes, if circumstances had been just a little different, she could very easily have been counted herself.

Marie Brennan is a former anthropologist and folklorist who shamelessly pillages her academic fields for material. She most recently misapplied her professors' hard work to the Victorian adventure series The Memoirs of Lady Trent; the first book of that series, *A Natural History of Dragons*, was a finalist for the World Fantasy Award and won the Prix Imaginales for Best Translated Novel. *Cold-Forged Flame*, the first novella in the Varekai series, came out in September 2016. She is also the author of the Doppelganger duology of *Warrior* and *Witch*, the urban fantasies *Lies and Prophecy* and *Chains and Memory*, the Onyx Court historical fantasy series, and nearly fifty short stories. She writes about worldbuilding at:
https://www.patreon.com/swan_tower.
For more information, visit www.swantower.com.

Patricia MacEwen is a physical anthropologist. She works on bones from archaeological sites and does independent re-search on genocide. She worked on war crimes investigations for the International Criminal Tribunal, after doing CSI work for a decade, and was once a marine biologist at the Institute of

Marine & Coastal Studies at USC. Rough Magic, first in a foren-sic/urban fantasy trilogy, The Fallen, is out from Sky Warrior Publishing. She writes mystery, horror, science fiction, and fantasy. Her hobbies include exploring cathedrals, alien-building via nonhuman biology, and trawling through history books for the juicy bits.

New York Times bestseller, **Jane Yolen** is often called "the Hans Christian Andersen of America." She is the author of over 360+ published books, including OWLMOON, THE DEVIL'S ARITHMETIC, and HOW DO DINOSAURS SAY GOODNIGHT. A graduate of Smith College, with a Masters in Education from the University of Massachusetts, she teaches workshops, encour-ages new writers, lectures around the world. Her books and sto-ries have won an assortment of awards—two Nebulas, a World Fantasy Award, a Caldecott Medal, the Golden Kite Award, three Mythopoeic awards, two Christopher Medals, a nomination for the National Book Award, and the Jewish Book Award, among many others. Six colleges and universities have given her hon-orary doctorates. If you need to know more about her, visit her website at: www.janeyolen.com

Our Amazing Backers...

Alex Jay Berman, Alyksandrei, Andrew Hatchell, Bruce Cohen, C.N. Rowen, Carol Mammano, Curtis & Maryrita Steinhour, D Franklin, Danielle Ackley-McPhail, David Edelstein, David Perlmutter, Debbie S Vasilinda, eSpec Books, Ian Harvey, Jakub Narębski, John Bowen, John WS Marvin, Joris Meijer, Kerri Regan, Kerry aka Trouble, Kris Smelser, Kristyn Willson, Lace, Linda A. Bruno, Mark Carter, Mark Lukens, Michael M. Jones, Michelle Gamboa, Nathan Turner, Paul R May, Rhel ná DecVandé, Robby Thrasher, Scott Schaper, SorchaRei, Stephanie Lucas, Steven Saus, Sunny and Ben Jackson, Svend Andersen, Tamara Slaten, Tasha Turner, Thomas Bull, Valentine Wheeler, Vespry Family